ECHO & LIV

ARCHERS CREEK #3.5

BY

GEMMA WEIR

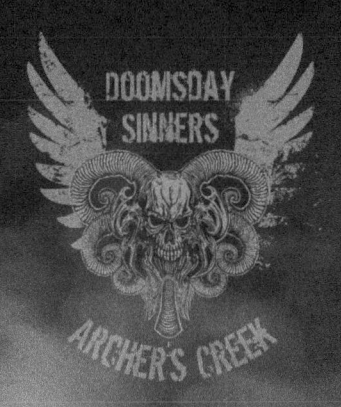

Echo & Liv

The Archer's Creek Series #3.5

Copyright © 2020 Gemma Weir

Published by Hudson Indie Ink

www.hudsonindieink.com

This book is licensed for your personal enjoyment only.

This book may not be re-sold or given away to other people. If you would like to share this book with another person, please purchase an additional copy for each recipient. If you're reading this book and did not purchase it, or it wasn't purchased for your use only, then please return to your favourite book retailer and purchase your own copy. Thank you for respecting the hard work of this author.

All rights reserved.

This is a work of fiction. Names, characters, places, brands, media, and incidents are either the product of the authors imagination or are used fictitiously. The author acknowledges the trademark status and trademark owners of various products referred to in this work of fiction, which have been used without permission. The publication/use of these trademarks is not authorised, associated with, or sponsored by the trademark owners.

Echo & Liv/Gemma Weir – 2nd ed.

ISBN-13 - 978-1-913769-93-2

*I'm totally dedicating this book to myself.
Echo is mine, and I wanted more of him.*

ONE

Echo

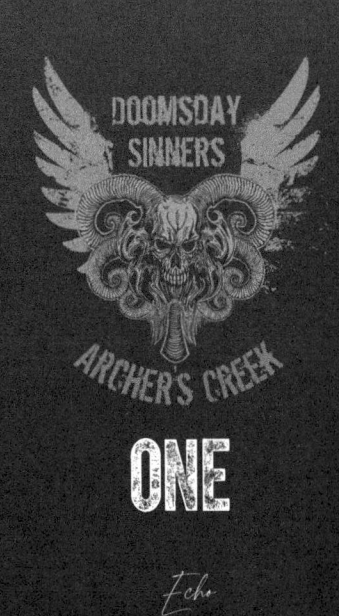

"Fuck you," Livvy screams from the top of the stairs.

I release a growl of frustration and clench my fingers into fists, reminding myself that I love my pain in the ass wife. With my jaw clamped closed, I attempt to inhale a calming breath… and fail. "Livvy, you've got two fucking seconds to get your ass down here, before I come up there and get you."

"Go fuck yourself, Echo," she screams again, and I hear the telltale sounds of her stomping across the landing, then the loud thud of our bedroom door being slammed shut.

Slowly turning away from the stairs, I force my feet in the direction of the kitchen. If I can give her a minute, we can both calm down. I take one step, then another; my teeth grinding, barely holding in the snarl that's building in my throat. I can't do it. My legs stop moving, then without thought, I spin and march in the opposite direction. I take the stairs two at a time and seconds later I'm in front of our bedroom door. Turning the handle, I throw the door open hard enough for it to ricochet off the wall and bounce back toward me.

My wife stands in the entrance of our closet. Her back is to me and her hands are fixed firmly on her hips. She's wearing nothing but a pair of pink lacy panties. The anger instantly drains from me and is replaced with pure unadulterated want.

"Livvy, come here," I growl, my voice low and full of intent.

"No," she says without turning to acknowledge me.

"Sugar," I warn.

She slowly turns her head to look over her shoulder at me. She must recognize something in my face because she pulls her lower lip between her teeth and nibbles at it nervously.

"Come here."

Her hands fall to her sides and she shakes her head.

"If I have to come over there, you might not like what's gonna happen."

I watch as her shoulders tense and her hands curl into fists. "I'm going to work, Echo, and there's nothing you can do to stop me."

"Try me," I say, my voice firm.

"I have my work permit. There's no reason why I can't go to work," she says, grabbing a tank top from the closet and pulling it over her head.

"Other than I said you can't."

With the tank covering her perfect tits, she spins to face me, anger flashing in her eyes. "I don't give a fuck what you say. I'm going to work. I have absolutely no intention of just sitting here on my bloody fat arse until this baby pops out. I finally got my work permit, so I'm going. To. Work. End of discussion."

"No. You're. Not," I say, slowly moving toward her.

Her eyes widen as I get closer, and she instinctually steps back. My cock twitches and I take another step toward her. She steps back again, and I follow her until her back hits the wall. Lifting my arms, I place my palms on the wall on either side of her head, caging her in with my body. "Nowhere to run, Sugar."

"Echo," she says, her voice wavering.

"Take off the tank."

"No."

I laugh. "You can take it off, or I can rip it off. Your choice."

"Or you could move your stupid fucking caveman self out of the way, so I can finish getting ready for work," Livvy cries, pushing at my chest and unsuccessfully trying to move me.

"I already told Brandi you weren't coming."

"You what?!" she screams, thumping my chest with her tiny fists.

Her eyes burn with anger and I can't help but smile. This woman is my life—my fucking world—but she must be batshit crazy if she thinks I'm about to let her go work in a bar when she's six months pregnant with my kid. Lowering my hands to her hips, I run my fingertips along the hem of her tank top and watch as she shivers at my touch. Lust replaces some of the anger in her eyes, and my cock pushes excitedly at my zipper. "Take. Off. The. Tank," I enunciate slowly.

She shakes her head as if she can shake off the lust that's pulsing through her. But she's lost the battle already and we both know it. A single touch of my skin to hers, that's all it takes. But she isn't ready to give up yet. I love how she fights it even though I know if I were to reach between her thighs I'd find her wet and ready. She still won't submit to me without a struggle.

I can see what she wants; it's so clearly reflected in her eyes. She can't hide the desire on her face, and we both know how this argument is going to end. But this is the way we are, the constant need to dominate her never goes away, and neither does her need to defy me.

"Move," she says, her hands shoving at my chest again.

Catching both of her arms, I slowly lift them above her head, holding them against the wall with one hand.

"Echo," she snaps at me, wrestling to free herself from my grip. "Let me go. You're such a fucking pain in the arse. don't want to play with you right now. I'm hot, I'm the size of a fucking beached whale, and I want to go to work. Why don't you give Sleaze a call and go do badass biker things for a few hours and leave me alone?"

I chuckle. "Badass biker things?"

Livvy humphs and twists her head until she's looking over

my shoulder and ignoring me. A spike of anger at her dismissive behavior pulses through me, and I move closer, until my body is surrounding her, and her pregnant belly is flush with my abs.

Her belly hiccups as our baby kicks, and all of my anger evaporates. Releasing her hands, I fall to my knees in front of her, sliding my fingers under the fabric of her tank and pushing it up and over the roundness of her stomach. Leaning forward, I place my lips against her skin and kiss her just above her bellybutton. Her sigh is audible, and I smile against her skin. "Hey in there, Princess. You being kind to your mama?" I whisper, as my hands caress her stomach, tracing the curve of her rounded belly.

"I thought she'd finally fallen asleep; she's been kicking the shit out of me all morning," Livvy says, all traces of her earlier anger now gone as well.

From my position on the floor, I look up at my wife's face and smirk. "My baby girl's strong and feisty, just like her mama."

Livvy scoffs, but her eyes never leave mine as I push up from the floor and stand in front of her again.

"I want to go to work, Echo," she says, determination in her voice.

"I know. But I don't want you on your feet behind a bar for hours on end while you're pregnant, Sugar. I already told Brandi that you wouldn't be working at Strikers, and I told Sleaze to make sure his woman understood, and not to put you on the rota no matter what you said to her."

"I'm pregnant, Echo, not ill. I'm more than capable of standing for a few hours and serving beers," she says, stamping her foot in frustration.

Gripping the fabric of her tank, I slowly run my thumbs in circles over her ribs. "I said no, Sugar. Why do you have to argue with me about everything?"

Fire sparks in her eyes again and a smirk twitches at the edge of her lips. "Because you like it when I fight you."

TWO

Libby

The words are out of my mouth before I even realise what I'm saying. Taunting him isn't going to get me any closer to going to work; and honestly, I'm already exhausted just from arguing with my pig headed, bossy man. Earlier, the idea of finally going back to the bar had sounded great, but now all I want is for Echo to rip down my knickers and fuck me.

Being pregnant is the biggest mindfuck I've ever had to deal with. One minute I'm furious, and the next I'm so turned on that I swear I could dissolve into a pool of horny mush. My body and mind have been taken over by pregnancy hormones and it's driving me crazy.

I need Echo to touch me, but I can't tell him that because then he will have won; and even though I'm desperate for him to fuck me, I also want to piss him off at the same time. See what I mean about the mindfuck?

He lifts my arms into the air again, holding both of my wrists with one of his enormous hands. "I do like it when you fight me, Sugar. But I like it more when I make you do as you're told."

Arousal pools in my stomach, and I fight to hold back a shudder as my body reacts to his voice and his touch. My top is pushed up, the fabric resting above my swollen belly and I watch his free hand slide up my thigh, across my stomach, until it reaches my shirt. He plays with the hem, his fingertips gliding close to the underneath of my breasts but not quite touching.

My nipples are hard and so eager to be touched. I arch my back, trying to push my aching tits into his hand and the tip of one finger grazes the underside of my breast. I gasp, silently willing him to do more, but he doesn't.

My eyes are riveted to him. He drops his head, pausing mere millimetres from my nipples, close enough I can feel the heat of his breath against my skin. He looks up at me and licks his lips.

"Echo," I rasp.

"Who do you belong to?"

I whine, the noise so full of desperation, I want to roll my eyes at myself. Two minutes ago, I was angry and ready to kick him in the bollocks, and now I'm panting for him like a dog in heat. I'm pathetic, but I'm also pregnant and horny, and so incredibly turned on by his possessive, alpha tendencies.

"I belong to you," I say, like I do every time he asks me this question. He owns me; heart, body, and soul, and I love the way his eyes darken when he claims ownership of me.

"Damn fucking right, you do. These tits belong to me," he growls, roughly cupping one of my aching breasts in his palm.

I groan loudly, and my eyes fall closed. His thumb and forefinger roll my nipple from side to side, and I bask in the pleasure he's giving me.

"This ass belongs to me," he says, releasing my breast and harshly grabbing my ass and squeezing.

"This pussy belongs to me," he rasps as he slides his hand off my ass and forces it between my legs; cupping my wet, pulsing pussy and rubbing the heel of his hand against my clit.

"God, yes," I moan, spreading my legs, urging him to do more.

"I own you. I have since the day you turned up in Archer's Creek."

"Uh huh," I agree, words failing me as I try to grind my needy pussy against his hand.

"I claimed you, chased you, put a ring on your finger, and a baby in your belly. You. Are. Mine."

"Yes," I say, as he pushes one finger beneath the fabric of my knickers and begins to tease the folds of my sex.

"I love you," he drawls against my ear as he pushes a single finger inside me.

"I love you."

"Sugar, I don't want you to go back to work."

I try to concentrate on his words, but the slow glide of his finger inside my sex distracts me.

"I don't want you to have swollen feet because you've been standing behind a bar all day. I don't want you to be exhausted because you're doing too much when your body is growing our little princess inside you."

My heart melts. "Echo," I say, the last remnants of anger evaporating at his words.

"You're doing the most important job in the world already, Sugar, you're protecting our baby. You and our princess are everything to me and I want you to be safe and rested and cared for."

The slow push and pull of his finger accompanies his words, and I moan from the heat of pleasure he's building within me. He adds a second finger, filling me and stretching me, all the while rubbing my clit as he moves.

"If you decide you want to get a job after the baby's here, then I'll help you find something; but right now, you're not going back to work. Do you get me, Sugar?"

I can hear his voice, but I don't process his words. My eyes are still closed, and I bear down on his fingers, pushing them deeper and groaning when the tingle of pleasure escalates into a torrent of sensation.

"Do you understand, Livvy?" he demands, his voice rougher than before.

I don't respond. Instead, I roll my hips and bite my lip as I wait for the tide of my impending orgasm to consume me. His fingers still, but I'm unwilling to let my orgasm fade, so I push down onto them harder. Echo's grip on my wrists loosens and all of a sudden, my arms are free, and his hand is cupping my chin.

My eyes snap open and I audibly groan, rolling my hips again and trying to ride his hand. His eyes narrow and he pulls his fingers from my pussy, leaving me empty and aching on the precipice of release.

"No," I cry.

A stinging slap against my clit has me crying out in pain, pleasure, and need.

"Do you get me, Livvy? No work until after the baby comes."

He slaps my clit again and my world tilts to the side. It hurts, but the pain splinters something inside me and all I can hear is the beating of my heart and all I can feel is need—pure unadulterated need.

"Livvy."

Echo's voice is louder, piercing the bubble of pleasure that's surrounding me.

"I need you and our princess safe. You're mine, and I'll protect you no matter what. Tell me you get me, Sugar. Tell me."

I nod, the movement jerky and frantic. Forcing my eyes open, I lock them with his. "I get you," I pant out.

The anxiety in his eyes settles and instead they fill with heat.

He leans forward and claims my mouth, devouring me with a kiss that's so full of love, possession, and dominance, that when he pulls away, I can barely breathe.

He slides two fingers back into me slowly, curling them so they tease my G-spot. My legs buckle, and I grind myself against his hand. "Please," I beg.

His fingers disappear, and I cry out, begging him incoherently not to stop. His palm slaps my clit and I jolt. He slaps it again and again, fast and hard enough that the sting of pain keeps me dangling on the edge of orgasm.

I scream in frustration and he rips my knickers to the side and roughly shoves two fingers into me. My orgasm splinters, throwing me into a torrent of sensation, and I scream. My legs buckle as I ride out wave after wave of overwhelming bliss that shatters me, until all I can see is stars, and all I can hear is the rasping pants of my breath.

My back hits the bed, the tank is dragged over my head and I hear the tearing of fabric as Echo literally rips my knickers off me. His cock fills me, and I scream again as my husband reminds me over and over why I should stay at home with him rather than go to work.

THREE

Echo

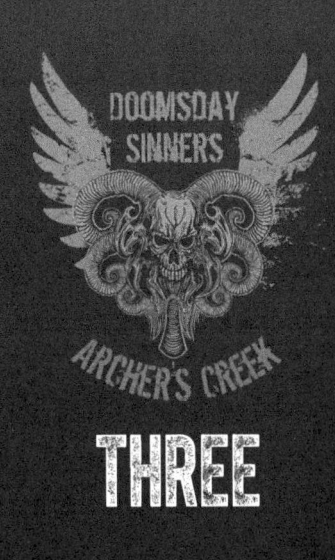

Livvy's nine months pregnant. Her due date was a week ago, and my beautiful wife is as pissed off as I've ever seen her.

Her body is full and womanly as she protects our baby girl inside her. She's fucking perfect. For every month that's passed I've watched her body change as she grows another fucking human being. She thinks she's ugly and fat; I think she's a fucking goddess.

"I hate you," she cries, tears running down her cheeks. "You did this to me, you fucking bastard. Look at me, I'm hideous. I'm so fucking fat I can't see my feet. My pussy's deformed and it must look like an eighties porno down there because I can't see to shave, and I doubt a beautician would be able to find it buried beneath my fucking belly."

"Livvy," I coo, trying to calm her down.

"Don't even fucking start, you dick. You're never coming near me with your cock ever again."

"Sugar, don't say stupid fucking shit like that."

"I'm serious. You did this to me, you and your stupid fucking caveman alpha bullshit. You knocked me up, so I wouldn't run again. But it backfired, you asshole, because look at me," she shouts, waving her arms up and down in front of herself.

I am looking, and my cock hardens almost instantly. Her tits are huge and full and round, her nipples have changed color and are big and pointy. Her hips are fuller, but still curved and begging to be held onto as I fuck her from behind. She's gorgeous and glowing, the most beautiful woman—the most perfect fucking thing this earth has ever seen and she's mine.

I stalk toward her and she holds a hand up in front of me. "I'm disgusting. I don't want a pity fuck, that's only going to make me feel worse about myself."

With a growl, I scoop her up into my arms and walk across the room, lowering her onto the dining table, her legs dangling off the edge.

"What are you doing?" she shouts, shoving at my shoulders.

"Livvy, shut the fuck up."

Her mouth closes with an audible pop, and I smile. "I have never, nor will I ever, pity fuck you." Grabbing her hand, I pull it over the bulge in my jeans. "My cock's been rock hard since the first time I laid eyes on you. Watching your body change, as you grow my baby inside you, is one of the sexiest motherfucking experiences of my life."

Her eyes hood, and I smirk in response. Hooking my fingers into the waistband of her shorts, I slowly pull them and her panties down her legs and discard them. "Lie back, Sugar," I order, my voice a growl.

Livvy lowers herself back until she's propped up on her elbows, her eyes never leaving mine.

"Spread your legs; I want to look at you."

Slowly, she lifts her legs and rests her heels on the table, then she lets her knees fall to the side revealing her wet, swollen pussy. "Fucking hell, I'm a lucky bastard."

Unzipping my jeans, I release my cock and step closer to her. I wrap my fingers around my length and squeeze tightly, then I brush the head over Livvy's clit teasing her and using her arousal to coat myself. Her muscles twitch and I place my free hand on the inside of her thigh spreading her legs wider apart until her cunt is fully on display for me. Rubbing my cock up and down her dripping sex, I torture both of us, then slowly push my cock between her folds. The heat of her pussy surrounds me and she clamps her muscles, strangling my length. She feels like perfection, but she isn't in control here. I freeze, not feeding her any more of my dick and wait. Within moments her hips are twitching and she's writhing beneath me. Smirking, I watch my beautiful wife's shocked expression when I pull my cock from her cunt, leaving her gaping slit empty and needy.

"Echo," Livvy moans, her back now flat on the table, her hands covering her eyes.

"What do you need, Sugar? Tell me. Ask me for what you want."

"I want you inside me."

"What do you want? Do you want my finger?" I ask as I slide a single finger into her wetness. Her pussy grips onto me tightly; the heat of her hot, wet channel making my dick even harder.

"No, I want your cock."

"You need to beg for it, Sugar. You told me you never wanted me to put my cock anywhere near you again, so beg me, Livvy. Beg me to fuck your pussy."

"God. Echo, fuck me. Slam your fucking dick into my cunt and fuck me. You own me, so take what's yours," she screams, her voice loud and needy.

My lips twitch into a smile, and I do exactly what she just begged me for. In one swift thrust, I fill her pussy up with my cock and start to fuck her.

Her orgasm hits the moment I'm seated fully inside her, and she screams. The sound is guttural and raw, and I clench my eyes tightly shut, to stop myself from following her into orgasm. "That's it, Sugar, take it. I own this cunt; don't ever tell me that I can't put my cock in you. Don't ever say you're ugly or fat. You're perfect and all, fucking, mine," I say, as I slide out and then plunge my cock into her tight, wet cunt once more.

With a grunt, I come, my hot seed pulsing into her pussy, filling her up. I fall forward, careful not to rest my weight on her stomach, and claim her mouth with mine. Kissing her, I swallow her gasps, then pull back and rest my forehead on hers. "I love you."

"I love you too," she says, her voice low and raspy.

Gemma Weir

FOUR

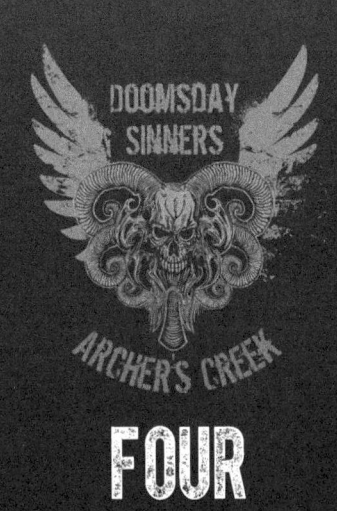

Livvy

After Echo fucks me on the dining table, he lifts me like I weigh nothing and carries me up to our bedroom. He strips me naked, then pulls me down onto the bed and climbs in behind me. Tears well in my eyes when his arm curls around me and rests on my swollen, incredibly pregnant belly.

Our daughter kicks her daddy and the gravelly sound of his laugh rumbles in my ear. "I fucking love you, Livvy."

I don't remember falling asleep, but that doesn't surprise me. Being this fat is exhausting, and our daughter is apparently a night owl. She kicks the most as soon as I climb into bed and although I can fall asleep at the drop of a hat, it's been weeks since I've slept for more than a couple of hours consecutively.

Our bedroom is dark, but I can see a sliver of light glowing beneath the bathroom door. I don't know if it's like this for anyone else, but since I hit the second trimester, if I even think the word bathroom, I need to pee. Carefully, I roll away from Echo's grip and with some effort, manage to right myself. My feet land on the floor at the side of the bed. The carpet is soft beneath me and I wiggle my toes into the deep pile.

My bladder tightens, reminding me that I need to pee, so I push up to standing and waddle across the room. I relieve myself, wipe, flush, and then wash my hands. Padding back into the bedroom, I glance at Echo asleep in the bed. I want to climb back under the covers with him, but agitation washes over me and turning my back on the bed I waddle over to where our clothes are dumped in a pile on the floor. Bending over, I pick up his jeans, shirt, and boxers as well as my bra and shirt, and start to straighten.

Before I'm upright, I feel a sudden surge of pressure and then a gush of warm liquid is running down my legs. "Oh my god," I cry, equally freaked out and disgusted.

Echo bolts upright in bed, scanning our room until he spots me. "What's the matter?"

"Either I just pissed myself, or my waters broke."

Echo's mouth falls open, and he gapes at me, unmoving, frozen to the spot.

A horrified laugh bubbles from me and I giggle maniacally until a dull, uncomfortable pain starts to build in the base of my spine. "Ohh," I say, reaching around to rub at my back.

The noise startles Echo, and he jumps from the bed, his cock still semi-hard and waggling around. He rushes to my side and takes the clothes I'm still holding from my arms and throws them in the direction of the clothes hamper.

"You okay?" he asks, fear lacing his voice.

Another gush of warm liquid runs down my legs and I look down at my wet skin and the darkening patch of carpet beneath me.

"What's going on, Sugar?"

I shake my head, looking between the floor and Echo and then back down to the floor. "I'm fairly sure my waters just broke."

"Fuck." Echo shouts, releasing me to rush to the dresser. His hands are a frenzy of activity as he pulls out pants and a shirt and quickly dresses. "Where's the duffel? We need to get you to the hospital."

I smile at his panic-stricken face. "My waters only just broke. I'm not even having contractions yet. I don't need to go to the hospital."

His face twists into a scowl. "You're having a baby; you need to go to the fucking hospital."

Laughing lightly, I waddle towards the bathroom, needing to clean up and get rid of whatever the liquid is that's still running down my legs. I gasp as another dull twinge pulls in my lower back. My belly tightens, and I rub one hand across my stomach while the other grips at my back.

"Oh fuck. Oh fuck. I need to get your stuff. We need to go to the hospital right fucking now."

The twinge fades and I start to move again, but Echo squeezes my arm, halting me. "What the fuck are you doing?"

"I'm going to get all this fucking baby juice off my legs and change my knickers. What the bloody hell do you think I'm doing?"

Before I know what's happening, Echo scoops me off the ground and into his arms.

"Put me down, you'll get covered in the baby juice too."

"I don't give a fuck. You're having a baby. You shouldn't be walking. What happens if the baby falls out?"

A bark of laughter escapes me and another gush of liquid leaks from me. "Urgh, Echo, don't make me laugh, I'm leaking."

"Oh fuck. Do I need to call an ambulance? Shit, what do I do?"

He finally lowers me to the ground in front of the bath tub and I lean forward to turn on the tap. "Honey, you're being a bit of a pussy," I say dryly. "I'm in very early labour. I need to take a bath and then ring the hospital to let them know that I'll be in sometime today or tomorrow."

"I'm not a fucking pussy. You can get cleaned up and then I'm taking you in."

Reaching forward, I test the temperature of the water with my hand and then push the plug into place. The bath starts to fill just as a dull pain twinges in my back. I rub at the base of my spine with my hand, ignoring my panic-stricken husband.

Without a word, he moves my hand out of the way and gently kneads my skin. My eyes fall closed, and a relieved sigh escapes my lips. "I'm taking you in, Livvy. Don't fucking argue with me, 'cause you know I'll get my way. You and our daughter are too fucking important to risk not getting checked out."

Any resolve I had to argue melts at his words. This man is so infuriatingly bossy and dominant, but on the flip side he's sweet and attentive and he loves me just as much as I love him. "Okay," I agree softly.

Warm lips touch my shoulder and I lean into them. His touch has always disarmed me. He's not always gentle, in fact some of my favourite times are when he's rough and demanding. But no matter what he's doing to me, I always crave more; more of him, more of his touch, more of his love.

Neither of us speaks while we wait for the bath to fill. Echo checks the temperature of the water several times and when it's full, he turns off the taps and holds out his hand to help me climb into the water. I shuffle forward, and he quickly strips and climbs in behind me, his strong arms holding me tight to his chest.

"I love you," he says, as he reaches for a sponge and starts to wash my breasts and the top of my stomach.

"I love you too."

He sits up and leans forward slightly so he can reach down my stomach, but I laugh and take the sponge from him when it's clear he can't reach any further. When my skin is clean and warm, Echo climbs out of the bath and carefully lifts me out. The pain hits when my feet touch the floor and I hiss at the tightness across my stomach, and the twinging in my back. Fear and panic begin to build. I'm in labour, actual proper labour, and in the next day or two my daughter will be here, and I'll be a mom. We'll be someone's parents.

Echo's face blanches, and he immediately starts to rub at my lower back like he'd done earlier. Within a minute the pain subsides. "You okay, Sugar?" he asks.

I nod. "Yeah, I'm fine. The pain's gone now. We're having a baby."

His lips twist into a smirk. "I know, Sugar."

"Fuck."

"You're gonna be just fine."

"With the labour yeah, but what about when the baby's here? I have no fucking clue what to do with a baby."

"Livvy, shut the fuck up. You're gonna be an amazing mom and you know it. Now let's get you dry, and I'll call the OBGYN to let them know we're coming in."

Forty-five minutes later, Echo practically carries me into the hospital while I try to breathe though the increasingly painful contractions. The pains are still far apart, but fuck they hurt. In the last hour-and-a-half since my waters broke, the intensity has built from a niggle to an 'oh shit this hurts' level of pain.

Echo pushes open the doors to the maternity department

and guides me through. Dr. Eidelman walks towards us, a huge smile on her face. "Mr. and Mrs. Stubbs, are we ready to have a baby today?"

Her enthusiasm annoys the crap out of me, but instead of telling her to shut the fuck up, I just smile and nod. Holding out her arm, she gestures for us to walk ahead of her and down a corridor filled with private labour suites. I never saw a maternity ward in the UK, but I'd lay bets that they aren't as posh as the one we enter. The walls are painted a soothing pale blue and the plush sofa is a warm cream colour. There's a T.V. playing Zen-like music videos on the wall, and a huge birthing pool fills one corner of the room.

Dr. Eidelman hands me a hospital gown and flashes me with her overly bright smile just as another contraction hits. My eyes search for Echo, and when he sees the pain on my face, he immediately moves to my side and rubs at my back. Unlike before, his touch is soothing, but does nothing to alleviate the pain, and I pant loudly as I try to breathe through the contraction.

"Well Mrs. Stubbs, by the looks of it your labor is progressing nicely. As soon as you feel able, if you could get undressed, slip on the gown and get onto the bed. I'll be back in just a few minutes to examine you and see how far along we are. With your first baby you could be in labor for a day, or a couple of hours, but usually when it's your first time it takes your body a while to really understand what's happening. If you need any help, just press the buzzer and a nurse will come in."

She smiles brightly with her blindingly white teeth and then leaves the room, closing the door behind her with a barely audible click. The pain of the contraction fades and I exhale slowly, trying to even out my laboured breaths.

"I want you to have an epidural," Echo rasps, his voice strained.

"No."

"I don't like seeing you in pain, Sugar."

"We talked about this. I don't need to get an epidural unless things get bad. I don't want a fucking great big needle stabbed in my spine unless I absolutely have to."

Sighing, he lifts my T-shirt, pulling it over my head and placing it on the chair beside the bed. I'm not wearing a bra and as I stand there topless, his eyes sparkle with desire. "I'm in labour, Echo, don't get any funny ideas. For the next few hours my pussy belongs to the baby that's trying to force its way out of there."

He scowls at me and I laugh. "You knocked me up, now you have to deal with the fact that my pussy will never be the same after your daughter comes out of it."

At the mention of our daughter, his face softens, and he steps into me and kisses me on the lips. "You grew our daughter inside your body and protected her for nine months, Sugar. You're amazing, and I'm prepared to relinquish ownership of your perfect pussy until she comes into the world. But the moment she's here, your pussy becomes mine again."

I laugh, because only my insanely possessive biker could make something as ridiculous as that sound sweet.

Gemma Weir

FIVE

Echo

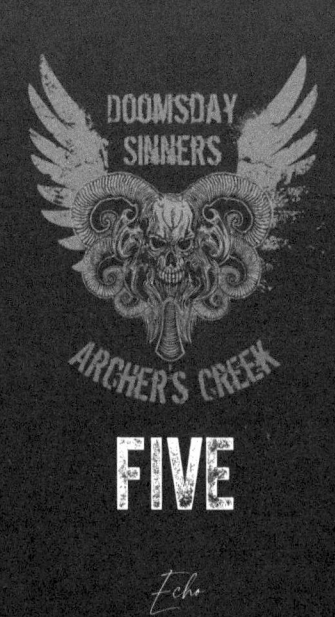

I help Livvy change into the ugly blue hospital gown and lift her onto the bed. The last time we were at this hospital was when she was attacked, and even though the circumstances are different I still fucking hate this place. The rest of her checkups have been at the doctor's office, and honestly, I don't know why she couldn't have just had the baby there. Her fucking uber perky doctor knocks on the door and then enters the room. Dr. Eidelman is blonde, looks to be in her early forties, and is a cheerleader type. Most people would probably love her, but honestly, she's starting to piss me off. My wife's in pain; what the fuck is there to smile about?

The doc walks to the side of the room and pulls on white latex gloves. "Okay then, Mrs. Stubbs, if you bend your legs and then let your knees fall to the side, I'll check how dilated you are."

Livvy does as she's asked, and I grip her hand tightly as the doctor bends over and examines my wife's pussy. Any man who tells you it's not awkward as fuck when a doctor has her hands up in your woman's cunt is fucking lying. I have no idea where to look. I can't watch the doctor mess with Livvy's pussy because that just seems beyond fucked-up, but I can't stare at the ceiling because that seems worse. So instead, I focus on Livvy's hand, and lift it to my lips, kissing it lightly before I give it a quick squeeze.

A few moments later the doctor straightens, still smiling widely. "Things are looking great. You're about four centimeters dilated, so almost halfway there. Did you make any decisions about pain relief? I can schedule an epidural if you'd like? Or we can think about alternatives once your labor is more intense."

"I don't want an epidural. I'm okay at the moment," Livvy says stubbornly.

The doctor's smile slips slightly, but she just nods. "Okay, well I'll leave you to get settled in, and I'll be back to check on you in a little while. You can stay in bed, or if you're feeling up to it, you can get up and walk around, whatever feels most comfortable. If you need anything at all just press the buzzer."

An hour later, Livvy is six centimeters dilated and her contractions are much closer together and much stronger. She's out of bed, her ass clearly visible through the back of her hospital gown as she paces a figure of eight at the side of the bed. I have no fucking clue what to do.

The sun is starting to rise, and my beautiful, vibrant wife has become the fucking antichrist. I've lost all the feeling in my right hand from where she squeezes the shit out of it every time a contraction hits, and over the last six hours I've learned that if I speak, Livvy will fucking scream at me.

"You fucking bastard. You and your fucking big dick did this to me. Neither of you are ever coming near me again. I swear, I will fucking rip your cock off if you ever try to stick it in me again."

Our doctor stopped smiling over an hour ago when Livvy threatened to punch her in the face if she didn't stop looking so fucking happy about how much pain she was in. I'm pretty sure the doc had tears in her eyes when she backed out of the room.

Silently, I push the hair out of Livvy's eyes and lift the bowl of ice chips closer to her hand. Her eyes lift to mine and I can see the pain is starting to overwhelm her. "Sugar, let them give you an epidural. Please. I don't like seeing you in this much pain when they can make it stop."

"No," she snaps, as another contraction hits and she slams her eyes shut and grits her teeth.

Nova May Stubbs finally arrives weighing 6 pounds, 5 ounces at 7:25am, and as she lies sleeping in her mama's arms, my heart fucking bursts with more love than I even knew existed.

"Thank you," I whisper as I lean down and kiss Livvy's lips. "She's fucking perfect; you're both fucking perfect."

Livvy's eyes never stray from our tiny daughter, but the smile that lifts at the corner of her mouth is all I need to see. A full minute later, her eyes finally lift to mine.

"We made her," Livvy says, her voice reverent and barely above a whisper.

"Yeah we did, Sugar. I love you both so much."

"God, I love you too."

SIX

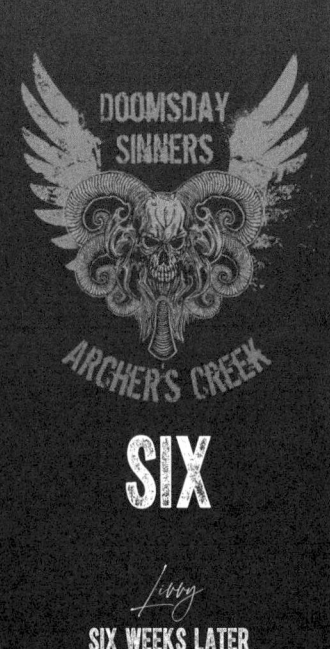

Libby
SIX WEEKS LATER

Tonight's the night.

Nova is six weeks old today, and although having a newborn is a baptism by fire, I wouldn't change a single moment. Her tiny fingers are curled into tight fists and both of her arms are raised above her head as she sleeps peacefully in her bassinet.

I tear my eyes away from her and glance around the room. Our home is now an explosion of pink. It turns out that the entire Doomsday Sinners Motorcycle Club morph into total softies when one of the old ladies has a baby. Every single member stopped by to meet her and they all carried pink stuffed animals, pink onesies, and a sea of pink clothes.

of every single badass member. The club has officially become my family and my little girl is incredibly lucky to have so many amazing uncles.

Echo walks through the door and immediately scans the room until his eyes lock on Nova. When he finds her, his face softens and his love for her is so clear that tears fill my eyes. When he's looked his fill, he crosses the room, pulls me into his arms and kisses me. I melt. It's been a long six weeks without his touch. I feel fine and have for a couple of weeks, but Echo was determined that he wouldn't touch me until after the six weeks recovery time the doctor told him I'd need.

Tonight's the night. Brandi and Sleaze are coming to watch Nova while Echo and I spend some much needed time together. Once we get back, I plan to seduce my husband and fuck his brains out.

Separating myself from his arms, I smile lovingly up at him. "I need to go get ready."

His arms lock around me and he pulls me back into his embrace. "You're mine tonight, Sugar," he drawls against my neck.

Looking up at him through my lashes, I bite my lower lip as lust plows through me. "I can't wait."

Echo growls. He actually growls, and my knickers are instantly damp. It's been months since I've heard that noise and God, I missed it. Pushing onto my tiptoes, I slam my lips against his. I love the moments like this, the ones where for just a second, I'm the one in control of our touch. But in the blink of an eye Echo takes charge. His fingers tangle in my hair and he moves my head so he can deepen our kiss. His tongue forces its way into my mouth, and my alpha man dominates me completely.

Like always, when I'm consumed and totally enthralled in his orbit, time seems to stand still. Everything around us fades to grey and all I can see, feel, and smell is him. His tongue tangles with mine and I groan against his mouth. His fingers tighten in my hair, and the twinge of pain has me arching my back and pushing my tits into his chest. I want to be as close to him as I can. I want to feel his naked skin against mine. I want him.

A keening cry from Nova's bassinet shatters the moment and we release each other. I take a step out of his orbit and immediately feel the loss of our connection. Nova's cries increase, and my breasts start to hurt and a knot forms in my stomach. I have no idea if it's normal to feel this sense of discontent at the sound of your baby's cry, but when Nova cries I feel it in every inch of me.

I step forward, eager to reach her, but Echo steps into my path stopping me. "I'll get her, Sugar, you go get ready."

I want to push him aside and go to my daughter, but I force down the feeling and instead nod and smile. He leans forward, cupping my jaw with his fingers and kisses me. His lips only touch me for a second, but that's all I need to settle the ache in my heart. I don't know how he knows exactly what I need, but he always does. It's like he senses my unease and then reacts, knowing that he's the only person who can make me feel better.

Reluctantly, I back out of the living room, my eyes fixed on the man I love and our tiny baby girl in his arms. I could watch them forever. I've never really seen the appeal of men holding babies, until Echo held Nova to his naked chest the first night we brought her home. Even exhausted and emotional, my pussy fluttered at the sight of his tattoos, while he held our perfect angel in his arms.

Sighing deeply, I take one last glance at them, then force myself to climb the stairs up to our bedroom. Nova's crib is next to the bed and a changing station is setup in the corner. So much has changed from the first time I walked into this room.

I shower quickly, then pad naked across the room to the wardrobe. Catching my reflection in the full-length mirror, I wince at the sight of my body. Stretchmarks ravage my skin, and my once flat stomach has a slight post-pregnancy pooch. My tits are huge, and lifting my hands, I cup them, feeling the weight and fullness.

"Sugar, my cock's so fucking hard for you."

Startled, I jump, spinning around to find Echo watching me from the doorway. His smirk is carnal, and I know that if he didn't have Nova in his arms, he'd be pushing my hands out of the way and taking over.

"It's been a fucking long six weeks, so if you want to go out tonight, I suggest you find some clothes right now."

"You've seen me naked plenty since Nova was born."

"Yeah, but I knew I couldn't touch. Today, I get to reclaim what's mine and I'm barely holding onto my control."

"It's been so long since I was yours, I think I've forgotten how it feels," I say, taunting him.

"Don't push me, Sugar."

"You like it when I push," I reply.

A feral growl snarls from his throat and I shiver with excitement. I need him to lose control. I need him to turn full blown caveman on me. He loves to command me, and I love it when he does. I've missed his dominant behaviour these last few weeks, and tonight I intend to get my man back.

Stepping further into the wardrobe, I slowly and deliberately bend forward to pull open my underwear drawer. We both know I'm putting on a show for him. We both know I'm trying to make him crack but neither of us acknowledges the game we're currently playing.

I barely look at the pair of knickers I choose. My eyes are forward, but all of my attention is focused on Echo behind me. Clutching the scrap of lace between my fingers, I reach for the matching bra. The air surrounding us crackles with intensity as I slowly push the drawer closed and glance over my shoulder at the man behind me. My eyes soften when they fall on our daughter, happily drinking from a bottle Echo is holding to her mouth.

"Wear a dress," he says, his voice rough and low.

My eyes fall closed for the briefest of seconds. His voice and the command in it always turns my body molten. Just like he ordered, I pick a navy-blue dress from the hanger and slowly turn to face him.

"Give me the panties, Sugar. You won't be needing them."

A smile slowly spreads across my face and I take a single step forward and drop the lace into Echo's waiting hand.

The doorbell rings and I instinctively twist my head in the direction of the front door. I can feel Echo's gaze still focused on me, and when I turn back to him his heavy-lidded eyes are full of barely contained need.

"Get dressed," he commands before he turns and leaves the room.

Thirty minutes later, we're seated in a booth at the only Italian restaurant in town. I love this place and even though Echo wanted to go to a nicer place in Houston, I'd begged him to come here instead.

The waitress smiles as she hands us menus. "What can I get y'all to drink?"

"A beer and a Margarita please," Echo says, his eyes never straying from me.

I glance at the waitress and she's eying Echo like he's the finest man candy. When she sees me glaring at her, she quickly looks away. "I'll be right back with those for you."

Echo's chuckle is low and full of amusement. "Calm down,

Sugar."

"She was looking at you like she wanted to eat you."

He slides closer, his hot palm gliding up my thigh. His hot breath tickles at my neck and I shudder. "Do you want to eat me?"

My eyes fall closed, just as his hand slides beneath my dress. I press my thighs together to halt his progress, but he nips at my neck with his teeth.

"Open your legs."

"We're in a restaurant." I say on a gasp.

"Do it now, Sugar."

The warning in his tone has my legs falling apart. But it's not fear that has me doing what he orders. If I told him I didn't want him to touch me, he would stop. No, I spread my legs because I love this game, I love our power exchange and the way he unashamedly owns my body.

The waitress returns with our drinks, but I barely see her as Echo's long fingers slowly caress between my legs.

"Wider," he demands against my ear.

I instantly spread my legs further and I'm rewarded with the rich sound of Echo's laughter against my neck.

"So eager."

I gasp at the first stroke of his finger along my sensitive flesh, and when he pushes one long finger into my pussy I almost combust.

"Easy, Sugar. Everyone of your gasps and sighs is just for

me. If anyone else gets to see it, or hear it, you won't get the pleasure you need. Instead, when I get you home, I'll bend you over the bed and spank you till your ass is red raw."

The slow, teasing push and pull of his finger and the words coming from his mouth, have me pulsating with desire. I grip the table firmly and bite at my lip, but I can barely keep in the desperate sounds that are building in my throat. "Take me home," I rasp out.

"Oh no, Sugar. You teased me earlier and now it's my turn. I want you wet and squirming by the time we leave."

"I'm already wet," I say, almost begging.

"I know, I can feel your arousal running down my finger. Fuck, I can't wait to taste you; I want you to come all over my tongue."

Groaning quietly, I reach for my drink with shaky hands just as the waitress arrives at the table.

"Are you ready to order?"

Echo orders for us both, his finger still slowly pumping in and out of me, teasing me. "Please," I breathe, when the waitress finally leaves.

"No, Sugar, I'm not gonna let you come yet. I'm gonna keep you right on the edge all night, then I'm gonna sink my cock into your greedy cunt and make you scream. I can't fucking wait."

His voice, his words, have me clenching my sex muscles around his finger. He slowly withdraws, and I wait for the inevitable tingling of pleasure as his finger fills me again, but it doesn't come. Instead, Echo trails a wet finger along the inside of my thigh. "Why are you stopping?" I ask.

"Because I can. Because I want to taste how sweet your wet cunt is, all swollen and ready to be fucked." Slowly, he lifts his finger to his mouth and I can see my arousal glistening in the lamplight. I watch as his lips part and his pink tongue dips out and licks along the tip of his finger. "Fuck, Sugar, I forgot how good you taste."

He licks his finger again and groans. "I need more, I can't get enough." His hand drops below the table again and he plunges one finger inside my needy sex. I clench around him, desperate to find the friction I need to push me over the edge, but he quickly withdraws and brings his finger to his mouth again. I watch him, my breath catching in my throat.

Right before his finger reaches his lips he pauses, and his eyes lift to me. "Do you want to taste yourself, Sugar? Do you want to know how amazing your wet cunt tastes?"

His tongue laps at his finger and a violent shudder runs through me.

"You want to suck all of your flavor off my finger don't you, Sugar? I can see it in your eyes."

I nod, and he smiles—a wolfish grin that promises me he's going to devour me and enjoy every moment. He runs his damp fingertip across my bottom lip and my tongue instantly dampens my skin, pulling the taste of my own arousal into my mouth.

I watch as Echo's eyes widen and fill with lust. Compelled

to push him further, I lean forward, take the tip of his finger into my mouth and suck lightly, swirling my tongue around the skin.

"Fuck, Sugar, watching you suck your juices off my finger is one of the sexiest things I've ever fucking seen. I want to lift you onto this table, pull up that dress and sink into your hot, wet cunt."

The rest of the meal passes in a haze of lust-filled teasing. Once our meals arrive, Echo alternates between eating his meal and playing with me. His fingers tease my sex, pushing me to the verge of orgasm and then stopping, only to begin all over again five minutes later. By the time we climb back into the truck, my arousal slicks the inside of my thighs and my pussy is needy and soaking wet.

"Do you want to go for a drink?" Echo asks.

"No, I want to go home. I need to go home, and then you need to get rid of Brandi and Sleaze, because I warn you I'm walking through the door and stripping my clothes off. I promise Sleaze will see me completely naked if you don't get them out of the door and your cock inside me in the next ten minutes."

Echo chuckles darkly. "Is that so, Sugar?"

"Yes! I'm not kidding Echo. I will divorce your ass if you don't fuck me soon."

He growls, and his fingers grab my chin roughly, turning me to face him. "That's not fucking funny, Olivia. I'm serious. Don't even fucking joke about that shit. Divorce doesn't exist in your world. You're mine."

The angry, hurt expression on his face makes my heart lurch. Shuffling across the bench seat in the truck I snuggle into his side. "I'm sorry. You've just got me so fucking horny and wound up. I need you."

Some of the anger leaves his shoulders, and I clench my thighs together and will him to drive faster. When our house comes into view, I open the door before he's even come to a stop. Dashing from the truck, I climb the steps and open the front door. Brandi and Sleaze are on the couch, Brandi's head resting in Sleaze's lap. She sits up when she sees me and a bright smile flashes across her face.

"She was an Angel. Princess Nova is fed, changed, and fast asleep in her crib. Love you, and I'll see you tomorrow," she says, as she quickly pulls Sleaze to his feet, before she winks at me and heads for the door.

"Love you too," I call to her back as she leaves. I don't stop moving as I unzip my dress and let it fall to the floor. Stepping over it, I climb the stairs to our bedroom, shedding my bra and dropping it as I push open the door and step into our room.

I hear Echo's heavy footsteps as he closes the front door and slowly climbs the stairs. My heart races, and my breathing gets shallow. Stepping across the room, I look into Nova's crib and lean down to kiss her perfect baby head. Her newborn smell hits me and instantly settles something within me. I'm still horny. I still need Echo and the pleasure I know he will give me. But this life, my husband and my daughter, they're everything, and in this moment, I feel so fucking lucky to have them.

When I look up, Echo is framed in the doorway. His shirt is off, fisted in his hands and hanging at his side. The lust and need are still there in his eyes, but the animalistic fire has settled. Neither of us needs to say anything because I know that he's feeling the same as me.

"I love you," I whisper.

SEVEN

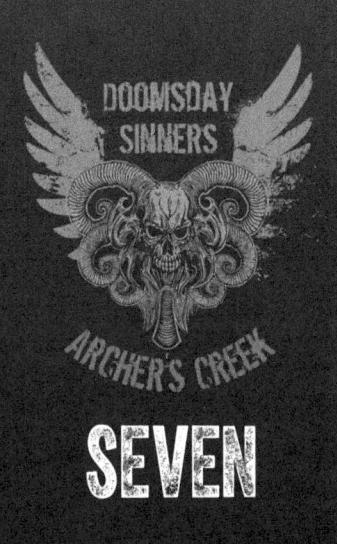

Echo

The desperation in her has faded, but her nipples are still pebbled, and I'd lay money on the fact that she's still wet and dripping for me. Sometimes I can't fucking believe this is my life, that she's my woman, my wife, and that tiny little baby girl is ours.

I'm the luckiest motherfucker on the planet.

I cross the room and stand next to Livvy. Nova's tiny fingers twitch in her sleep and I lean over and kiss the top of her head lightly. She lets out a snuffly breath and an overwhelming sense of peace settles over me. In this room is everything I'll ever need, and I silently promise to love her and her mama every day for the rest of my life.

Dragging my eyes away from my princess, I turn all my

attention to Livvy. Heat flares back to life in her eyes and I watch her chest rise and fall faster as her breath quickens.

"Get on the bed."

She stares at me for a moment and then scrambles onto the bed.

"Hands and knees."

She complies immediately and my cock pulses. Her ass is facing me, her pussy wet and shiny, just begging for me to kiss it and lick it and fuck it. "Knees wider. I want to see all of you."

Her ass swings from side to side as she edges her knees further apart. My cock is so hard it hurts, but I take my time undoing the fly of my jeans and stepping out of them. Anticipation is everything and I love it when she gets so mindless, so needy that she's blind to anything except me and what I'm going to do to her.

As I watch, she squirms, shaking her sex at me. Her neck is bent, and she's watching me watch her. When I finally step forward, she heaves a sigh of relief and drops her head. I run my hands down her ass, caressing the smooth skin. Curving around her thighs, I slide both of my thumbs along her wet folds and she pushes back into my touch. "It's been too long, Sugar," I croon to her.

"I know," she says, her voice raspy and low.

Lowering my face between her legs, I slowly slide my tongue from her clit, all the way up to her tight puckered asshole. Livvy gasps and then moans loudly. The sound of her pleasure makes me lose my mind and I feast on her, licking, sucking, and kissing until she's riding my tongue and chanting.

"Oh, God. Oh fuck, Echo. Oh my god."

Spearing her with two fingers, I suck on her clit until she detonates around me. Her pussy clamps down on my fingers and my cock almost explodes. I want inside her, I need inside her. Now.

I lay one last kiss against her clit and withdraw my fingers. Licking them clean, I slap Livvy's ass and she giggles. "On your back, Sugar."

Her movements are slow, her body languid and relaxed from the orgasm I just gave her. She opens her arms for me and I crawl up the bed until I'm lying between her legs. Leaning in, I kiss her, and she wraps her arms around my neck and clings to me. "I love you, Livvy, so fucking much."

Tears fill her eyes, but she smiles as she speaks. "I love you too."

Lining up my aching cock with her pussy, I slowly push inside her. Livvy's eyes roll to the back of her head and she grips me tighter as I fill her completely. "Wrap your legs around me."

With her arms and legs holding me, I slowly pull out, until only the tip of my cock is inside her heat, then I push back in. I kiss her as I thrust in and out of her and the feel of her hot, wet pussy almost undoes me, but I clench my teeth and ignore the need to blow my load.

I need to make her come before I'll allow myself to follow

her into oblivion. Slower than I'd like, I fuck her, our eyes locked, silent apart from her quiet gasps of pleasure. "You okay?" I ask, needing to make sure she's okay and not hurting.

"Yes. Oh God, Echo, it feels so good. Harder, please fuck me harder."

Thank fuck, I think to myself, barely keeping the words from escaping. Pulling out, I thrust back into her with a little more force and she arches her hips and rocks against my cock, pushing me to take her deeper.

My breathing becomes erratic and I start to lose control. My balls are full and heavy, and I need to come more than I've ever needed to come before. It's been six long weeks since I fucked my woman and my inner caveman is screaming at me to reclaim what's mine, to mark her with my seed and prove to everyone that she belongs to me.

Her pussy tightens around my cock, so I drop one hand between us and rub at her swollen clit. From the first touch she cries out and her pussy clamps down harder, her muscles starting to flutter as her orgasm builds.

I fuck her with earnest, all pretense at control lost as I slam my cock into my woman, again and again. I feel the moment she reaches orgasm and I thank the gods because I doubt I could have lasted a moment longer. She splinters around me; her cries of pleasure so loud that I kiss her to swallow the noise. My cock twitches and I explode, filling her with my cum, until we're both spent and exhausted.

Her legs and arms fall back to the mattress and I roll to the side to avoid crushing her with my weight. She crawls into me and I hold her sweaty body to mine, then like always, I reach between her legs and use my fingers to push the cum that's dripping between her thighs back into her sex.

EIGHT

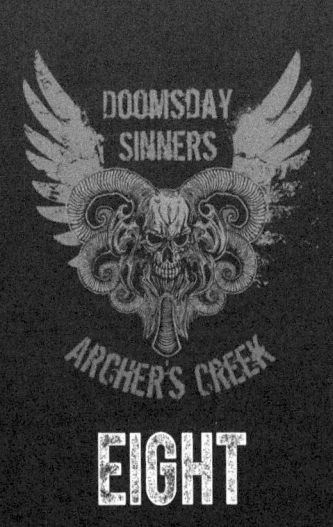

Livvy

It took fourteen weeks after Nova was born for Echo to get me pregnant again. It wasn't what we planned—in fact the birth control pills I was taking were supposed to have stopped it from happening—but fate obviously had other plans.

Zeke Milo Stubbs was born at a healthy seven pounds nine ounces and was the spitting image of his father. My babies are my absolute world, but with two children so close together I was shutting up the baby-making shop.

Unfortunately, fate never got the memo that time either, and a year after Zeke was born, my birth control failed again, and I fell pregnant. Leo Nathaniel Stubbs and Dillon Zander Stubbs were born four weeks early, weighing five pound one, and five pound two respectively. The twins are completely identical and look so much like Echo and Zeke that no one could ever fail to see the family resemblance.

After the twins' birth, I refused to let Echo near me until he got a vasectomy. He wasn't happy about it, but he went and got the procedure.

And so, life went on. We were a family; we were happy... until we weren't.

NINE

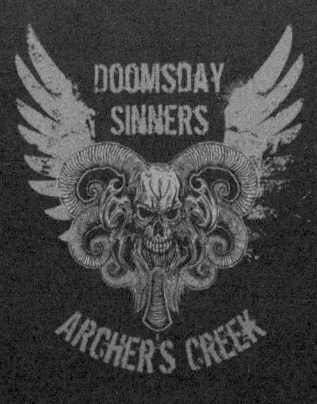

Libby
TEN YEARS LATER

"Nova, Zeke, Leo, Dill, get your arses down here."

"It's ass, Mom," Leo shouts.

"Leo, if I hear you say ass again, I'm gonna come up there and kick yours. Now all of you get downstairs. If you don't hurry up, you're gonna miss the bus."

The stairs pound as four sets of feet rush down them. Nova is the first to enter the kitchen, wearing tiny denim shorts and a white crop top. "Yeah, nope." I say, shaking my head. "Princess, turn your butt around, go back upstairs and put on some proper clothes. You're thirteen, not thirty, and you're not leaving this house with that much skin on display," I say, pointing my finger back towards the stairs.

"Mom, everyone at school dresses like this. I'm not a little girl and you're forcing me to dress like a baby."

"I know for a fact that your Uncle Blade would not let Emmy out of the house dressed like that, so don't give me that crap. Go get some clothes on. *Now*."

Nova huffs and turns to leave. "I hate you," she shouts as her feet stomp back up to her bedroom.

My heart thuds at the insult and tears fill my eyes, but I push back the emotion as my twin tornados rush at me. Leo and Dillon are my babies; at almost nine they're my youngest and most energetic kids.

"Mom, Mom, Mom," Leo shouts, at the same time as Dillon yells "Mama, guess what Leo did?"

They both throw themselves at me, and I pull them in for a hug. I never miss the opportunity of a cuddle from them because pretty soon they won't want to hug their mom, just like their older siblings.

"Okay, shush. Now Leo spoke first, so what do you need to tell me?"

"Mom, Dill said I took his pants. But I didn't, these are my pants."

I look down at the ripped skinny jeans my son is wearing and roll my eyes. I turn to Dillon, "Are you planning to tell me Leo stole your pants?"

Dill looks up at me, his expressive sky-blue eyes so different from his brother's dark navy-blue ones and nods. "They're mine, and I look cool in them, so Leo can't wear them."

Pulling in a reaffirming breath, I smile at them both. "Don't you remember when we went shopping for these pants? You both loved them, so I got you each a pair."

The boys stare at me for a long moment, then turn and look at each other. The similarity in their faces is unnerving sometimes. They're so identical that if they didn't have different eye colours I'm not sure even I could tell them apart. They start to giggle and then Leo shoves his brother and they break away from me, pushing each other and chattering as they make their way to the breakfast table to eat their cereal.

Zeke is the last to appear; his long brown hair hanging in his face and obscuring his eyes. "Morning, Ma," he says, his voice tired and slow.

Crossing the room, I push the hair from his face and lean in to kiss his cheek. Mornings are the only time he'll let me do this, when he's too tired to care. "Hey, baby," I coo. "You need a haircut."

He grunts, before sliding into a seat at the table and devouring his breakfast. Nova reappears, her hair pulled up into a messy bun and the white crop-top replaced with a vintage Nirvana T-shirt knotted at the side. She glares at me and throws her hands into the air dramatically. "Are you happy now? I look like a granny. Tyler Lawson's never going to notice me dressed like this."

"Who's Tyler Lawson? And how many grannies have you

seen in a Nirvana shirt?"

The twins chuckle in between shovelling food into their mouths. Zeke lifts his head, pushes his hair out of his eyes and glares at his sister. "Tyler won't be noticing you, 'cause if he does I'm gonna beat the crap out of him."

My oldest son is the spitting image of his father, in both looks and attitude. My heart pangs as I remember how caveman and possessive Echo used to be.

"Zeke, I swear I'll kill you if you say anything to Tyler," Nova shrieks.

Zeke chuckles menacingly. "Then make sure he stays away from you and I will. Dad said I'm responsible for keeping boys away and that's what I'm doing. Plus, Tyler's a loser."

"He's not a loser! And you're only twelve. Tyler's a full year older than you, he'd kick your ass," Nova shouts, her hands locked on her hips indignantly, a smug sneer plastered across her beautiful face.

Zeke smiles, and Nova's smug expression fades as he pushes back from the table and stands. Her eyes follow his assent until she's looking up at her younger brother. There's only a year between the two of them but Zeke is already taller than his sister. Unlike many of the kids in his grade, he's muscled and toned from all the football he plays, and from working out with his father and uncles. At only twelve he's already imposing, so he's going to be huge by the time he turns eighteen. Poor Nova, she'll never get a boyfriend.

"God, I hate you too," Nova cries, shoving Zeke in the chest before slumping down at the table.

Zeke turns to me and winks, then sits back down to finish his breakfast. I swallow a laugh; my eldest son is a quiet force to be reckoned with. His calm exterior hides the bubbling volcano within him. God help the first girl that pulls his interest.

While the kids eat, I pack up the twins' lunches and zip them into their backpacks. The older two eat in the school cafeteria, but my twins have too much energy to sit still long enough to eat, so they take a packed lunch, and I cut everything up small enough so they don't choke when they shovel the food into their mouths.

I check my watch; the bus is due in five minutes. "Bus is gonna be here in five minutes. Does everyone have everything they need?"

There's a chorus of yeses, but I've heard it all before, so I turn to my weekly organiser chart pinned to the wall and call off the kids' activities. "Zeke, you have practice tonight, so either me or your dad will pick you up at six. Nova, do you have that permission slip I signed for your class trip? Leo, Dill, I have a teacher conference with your teacher today, so best behaviour."

"Cool," Zeke says, grabbing his backpack and dropping a kiss to my cheek as he passes.

"It's in my purse," Nova tells me, rolling her eyes dramatically before she slides huge black sunglasses onto her face and hangs her purse over her arm.

"We'll behave," Dill says.

"Or at least we'll try." Leo replies, as they rush at me and wrap their little arms around my waist. They hug me tightly before they take the backpacks I'm holding out for them and rush out the door.

Like every day, I move to the front of the house and watch as Zeke and Nova wait for their younger brothers, and the four of them walk down the street to where the yellow school bus is just pulling in to pick them up.

"Hey, did I miss the kids?" Echo asks as he saunters down the stairs.

"Yep," I reply curtly, not taking my eyes from the window. I know they'll be fine, but no matter how many days they do this exact same thing, I always watch until they climb the bus steps.

The older kids go to the middle school, while the twins are still at the elementary school, but in a town this small they all ride the same bus. As soon as the doors close, I head back into the kitchen and find Echo pouring himself a cup of coffee from the pot already made in the corner. We don't speak, and I busy myself cleaning up the breakfast things and loading them into the dishwasher.

"I'm gonna be back late. I've got six sites to visit today, and I need to go to the club tonight."

I nod silently. This shouldn't surprise me, he's been at the club every night for months.

So much has changed since we met. He swept me off my

feet and bulldozed through all of my reservations. The start of our relationship wasn't easy, but I fell for him and his dominant charm. I barely recognize the people we are now. We used to be inseparable, incapable of staying away from each other, but now we barely speak, living separate lives under the same roof. I never imagined I'd end up with a biker, but the club became my family and the Sinners were as much a part of my life as they are his. But that's not how it is any more. We don't go to the club together now—I stay home, and he goes alone. I get it, it's not like we can take the kids to the club on a night-time. Watching the members get head or hearing the screams of delight as a few of the guys tag team one of the club girls on the pool table, isn't exactly a kid-friendly activity.

I miss it. I miss the parties. I miss how possessive of me Echo would get when we were there. How he would insist I sat on his lap, so no one would mistake that I belonged to him. I miss my extended family, because when Echo and I drifted apart I didn't just lose him, I lost the club too.

When I first came to Archer's Creek, I worked at one of the bars the club owned, but after Nova was born and falling pregnant so quickly again with Zeke, I never went back. With two small children, the thought of going back to work never really crossed my mind. Then the twins came along and paying for four lots of daycare seemed absurd, especially when Echo's wages could comfortably support us all.

About a year after the twins were born, I started to get stir crazy and decided to go to night school. It took me five years and a whole lot of sleepless nights, but I'm now a fully qualified certified public accountant. The moment I finished my CPA course, Anders asked me to take over the club's books, and with all the businesses they own, they keep me pretty busy. Echo built an addition onto the house, giving me an office, and the twins each their own room; and now I work from home while the kids are at school. You would think that working for the club would make me feel closer, a part of the family again. But instead it did the opposite. The Sinners are my employers and I feel more disconnected from them than ever.

I shouldn't complain, life is good.

Except it isn't.

I'm lucky. I have four amazing kids, a good job, and a beautiful home. But I miss my husband. We're still together, we still sleep in the same bed every night, but a few years back something changed. I can't put my finger on what exactly is different, but the dynamic between us altered and although I'm not unhappy, I'm not happy either.

I'm lonely. I live in a house full of people, but I'm lonely.

"See you later," Echo says, brushing a kiss over my cheek absentmindedly as he walks past me and out of the door. I hear the click of the front door closing behind him, and only then do I let the single tear fall down my cheek. I only ever let one tear fall. I've got too much to be happy about to mourn the loss of something I can't even identify.

When I feel the wetness roll down my cheek, I reach up and wipe it away.

Gemma Weir

TEN

Echo

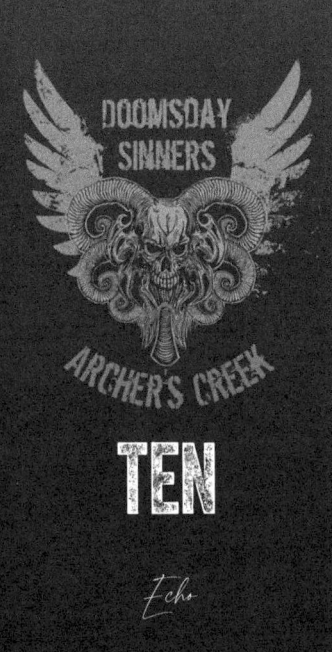

This day has been a fucking nightmare. Every site visit had more and more problems and now hours later when I'm pulling into the club compound, I'm ready to say fuck it and go home to my wife and kids.

Someone's fucking with the club. Security sites vandalized, construction sites delayed by red tape and zoning bullshit. Even the illegal side of things is going to shit, a delivery of fertilizer was tampered with and we lost an entire crop of top-quality weed. All in all, everything is a fucking shit show at the minute.

To make matters worse, something's wrong with Livvy. Everything had to change when we had the kids; we couldn't both be at the club every night with a brood of babies in tow. Then she decided to go back to school and for fucking years she lived and breathed schoolwork, diapers, and pretty much nothing else.

I'm not complaining. I'm so fucking proud of her. She's an amazing mom—our kids are fucking perfection, and that's all because of her. She managed to get her CPA qualification in record time while raising four small kids and looking after my fucking pain in the ass self.

But through it all we still managed to make time for us, up until the last couple years. I don't know what happened, but at some point, without me realizing it, we drifted apart.

I don't remember the last night we spent together. About six months ago, Anders closed ranks at the club. Only long-term members even know that the club's having problems. Prez was clear: no newbies, no old ladies, and no outsiders. I hate keeping shit from Livvy, but I won't betray my club, so this is just the way it has to be.

Every night for months we've been in church, hashing out the problems and trying to pinpoint who's fucking with us, and I finally think we have it figured out.

I kill my bike's engine and take the keys from the ignition. Climbing off, I eye the bikes in the lot, knowing from sight exactly which of my brothers are here tonight. The burble of a bike engine and the crunch of gravel beneath tires grabs my attention, and I turn to find Sleaze pulling in behind me.

Pausing, I wait for him to catch up with me and then we both walk toward the door together.

"I'll be glad to get this shit sorted," Sleaze says, his voice as gruff and low as always.

"Me too. I got shit I need to sort at home."

"The kids okay?" he asks, concern in his face.

"Yeah, they're fine. It's Liv."

Sleaze stops and puts a hand out to stop me. "She okay? Brandi never mentioned anything."

I rub a hand down my face and exhale. "She's okay. But we aren't. I don't know what's going on, but these last few years have been hard on us. I need my wife back."

Sleaze nods like he knows exactly what I mean. "What you gonna do?"

"Not sure yet, but I've had enough of this distance bullshit."

"I get you, Brother. Schools out for summer next week, so why don't the kids come with us when we head out? We've got a cabin booked in Big Bend National Park. The kids would all have to share, but there's more than enough room for them."

"You serious?" I ask.

"Course. Not like it's the first time we've all been on vacation together," Sleaze replies.

"Fuck. If you're serious, that would be perfect. A full week of just me and my woman. Sounds like heaven. Let's go get this shit sorted for the club, and I can go home."

With a renewed sense of purpose, I stride toward the clubhouse. The bar's quiet with only a handful of the regular club girls and the prospects playing pool, laughing, and drinking.

I envy them their carefree attitudes. Sleaze and I nod at them as we pass, but we don't speak. Instead, we make our way to church and the rest of our brethren.

As we push open the door, the oppressive tension that's constantly permeated the room for months now, hits me. Tonight, it feels worse; thicker and more dangerous. Sleaze and I move to take our seats, and as I scan the room, I realize we're the last ones to enter except for one chair that's still empty.

Axle's chair.

I pause, stunned for a moment as I stare at the empty chair. My gaze turns to Anders' and when our eyes lock, I know that I was right, that Axle was our rat. He was the reason our security was being sabotaged. He was the reason we were being hampered by red tape and zoning issues on construction sites that shouldn't have been affected.

"Why?" I say. The word slipping from my mouth before I can think better of it.

Axle's a legacy. He's been a member his whole life. Hell, he's in his sixties now; he's been part of the club since the day he was born and his daddy brought him out to meet his club brothers.

Anders motions to my seat, and I quickly slide into it. All eyes turn to our president and it's only then I see the strain in his face and the grief in his eyes. Axle was Anders' friend, his brother for decades. The room falls silent and we all hear the deep inhale Prez takes, and watch as he steeples his fingers and rubs at his temples with his thumbs. "There isn't a man in this room I wouldn't call my brother, my family. There isn't a single one of you I wouldn't die for."

He lifts his face and makes eye contact with each of us in turn. "The Sinners are my home. I've been a member all my life, and today is the only day that I've ever been ashamed to call myself a part of this institution."

Anders' voice cuts through the silence like a knife and his words make the air catch in my throat. I want to turn and look at my brothers' faces, but I can't; my eyes are glued to Anders, waiting for him to speak again.

"Over the last few months, we've been betrayed, sabotaged, and fucked with. As President of this club, I decided to close ranks, to exclude all but my most trusted family. Today, I found out with complete certainty who desecrated the bond of brotherhood. Today, I found out who pissed on our family, who disregarded decades of membership and loyalty. Brothers, men, today I broke my fucking heart."

In a room full of thirty men, you could hear a pin drop. No one speaks, no one breathes.

"There's one chair empty today. Over a decade ago, another member of our club betrayed us. Some of you won't remember a prospect called Slow. He sold out a member's old lady; put her in danger for a measly few thousand dollars. He was excommunicated from the club and exiled from the town. That prospect was Axle's son. Axle was the one who stripped him of his colors. He was a legacy, a proud member of the Sinners, and he disowned his son for his betrayal."

Anders pauses and drops his head into his hands for a second. When he lifts his gaze to the room once more, his eyes are red and full of emotion.

"I confronted Axle today. I begged him to deny he was the one who was betraying us. But instead he told me that he hated us, that the club had taken his only son from him. Slow died of an overdose earlier this year and Axle blames us—this club and his brothers. He decided to avenge his son's death by quietly destroying our livelihood. He planned to ruin one business after the next until the club was bankrupted. He never expected to be discovered, assuming no one would ever suspect him."

Murmurs of discontent rumble through the room full of men, and I watch as my brothers turn outraged eyes on one another. The thud of Anders' fist hitting the wooden table silences us once again.

"This is not how our family works." Anders shouts.

"We are loyal."

Bang, his fists hit the desk again.

"We are united."

Bang.

"We are a brotherhood."

Bang.

"We do not betray each other, or our club," Anders bellows, rising from his chair.

"We are not disloyal," he shouts, bringing both of his fists down onto the table with a crash.

I watch my president, his chest rising and falling erratically. His eyes are full of emotion and heartbreak, and my heart shatters for him.

Anders' head falls forward for a second and when he lifts it again, there's resolve in his features. "A man I've called my brother for over thirty years, laughed while he told me all he'd done to try to destroy us. He ripped his patch from his cut and threw it in my face. I left him with the intention of letting you, our club, decide how we should deal with him. But an hour ago, I received a call from the sheriff's office. At 4pm today, Axle put his gun in his mouth and killed himself."

No one speaks, but the sound of men shifting in their seats feels louder than if they were all shouting at once.

"Today is a day I want you all to remember. Today is the day that you receive a get-out clause. When each of you accepted your toprockers, you agreed to a lifetime of membership in this club. You committed to a lifetime of loyalty and allegiance, and in return you gained a family and a home. Many of you have lived in this clubhouse, some of you still do. The club provides you all with an income in exchange for your service and all we ask in return is for fealty, loyalty, and integrity. Tonight, I give you the choice to leave."

A cacophony of movement and shuffling feet fills the previously silent room.

"I would call every single man in this room my brother, but

if you don't feel the same, stand up and leave. There will be no retribution. If you leave tonight, you will forfeit your membership and you will no longer be a Doomsday Sinner. If you choose to leave, then take off your cut and get out. Hell, you can even stay in the fucking town; I don't care. What I do care about, is feeling like I can't trust my fucking family," Anders says, tension emanating from every inch of him.

My eyes scan the men to my left and right, and I find them doing the same. No one speaks, and no one stands to leave. My heart hammers in my chest, and for a single moment, I consider what my life would be like if I wasn't a Sinner anymore. An image builds in my mind, but the moment it starts to clear, I picture Livvy on the back of my bike in her property cut. I see my kids running around the club on family days, surrounded by my brothers' children. Anders is right; this club is my family, as intertwined with who I am as everything else that defines me.

Pushing back my chair, I rise to standing, and feel, rather than see, all eyes go to me. Anders' jaw tightens into a firm line, but I can see the shock he's trying to hide. I lock eyes with his. I want him to know—to see—that what I'm about to say is the God's honest truth. "I don't need a fucking get-out clause. I'm a Sinner. Dead or alive, here or not, that won't ever fucking change. You are my brother, my family. I'm a motherfucking Sinner and Sinner's look after their own." I clench my hand into a fist and thump it over my heart where my patch is. Then I sit back into my chair and fold my arms across my chest.

I watch as the tension bleeds from Anders' shoulders. His jaw relaxes and the hint of a smile flickers at the corner of his mouth.

Blade stands next. "I don't want a get-out clause. I'll be a Sinner until I take my last fucking breath."

Sleaze follows him. "I'm a Sinner and I'll die a Sinner."

Daisy stands. His woman is like a daughter to Anders and I know Prez thinks of Daisy like a son. He locks eyes with Anders and speaks. "You're my family, this is my home. I'm a Sinner and my sons will be Sinners."

One by one, each member rises and confirms his allegiance to the club. No one asks to leave, no one wavers. We're a club, and although Axle's betrayal might have cracked something, it won't fucking break us.

After the last man thumps his fist over his patch and sits back down, Anders looks at each of us in turn again. "I'm proud to call myself a member of this club. I was born a Sinner, my daddy was a Sinner, and when I came to the Archer's Creek chapter I knew I'd found my home. I'm proud to call you my brothers. But hear me loud and fucking clear, today was your one and only chance to walk away. If I ever find out that a member of this club has betrayed us, has dishonored our club, our family, then I will fucking find you and I will kill you myself. Do you understand?"

One by one we each nod our understanding and then Prez slams his fist down on the table. "We're done here."

The silent room bursts into sound as thirty men all scrape chairs and stomp feet as we make our way out of church, free of the oppressive tension that filled the room. As I reach Anders, I pause and squeeze his shoulder. "I'm sorry, Boss."

He turns to look at me and dips his chin, the grief clear in his eyes and the slight slump in his shoulders. "Me too."

Dropping my hand, I follow the rest of my brothers as we all file into the bar. Blade, Sleaze, Daisy, and a few of the others, drop into a group of sofas and I do the same. The vibe is somber, and no one wants to be the one to lighten the mood.

"Fuck this shit, I'm going home to my woman. I need to lose myself in my angel for a few hours," Daisy says as he rises from his seat.

We all nod in understanding and he slaps Blade's shoulder as he leaves. A dull ache forms in my chest. It takes me a moment to realize it's jealousy. I'm not jealous of his wife, but I am jealous of his surety that he'll be welcome.

It's been months since Livvy welcomed me with open arms and legs. Fuck, I don't even remember the last time she was awake when I got home. It's time to change that. Our lives might have changed—evolved—but I still love my wife like I did the day I married her. Anger and fear burn in my gut because I don't know if she still feels the same way about me. I refuse to lose her, so if she's forgotten that she loves me, I need to remind her.

With a renewed sense of purpose, I say goodbye to my brothers and head home to my wife.

ELEVEN

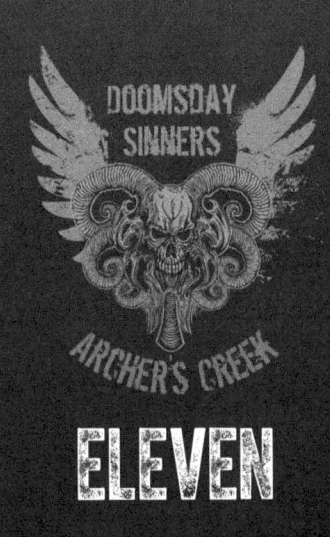

Livvy

I hear the front door open and close. I'm lying awake in our bed, waiting for him to come home. I do the same thing every night, but then I pretend to be asleep when he climbs in beside me. It's pathetic, I'm pathetic. But I can't help it.

I'm waiting for the day that he comes home smelling like club slut perfume. Echo is a highly sexual guy, and I know he's not getting it from me, so he's got to be getting it from somewhere. The thought makes my stomach fill with acid. Nausea rises in my throat, and I have to breathe through my nose so I don't give in to the need to vomit.

I'm such a cliché. The stupid little wife waiting at home while her husband cheats on her. I want to confront him, but I'm more terrified of having him confirm his betrayal, than I am of staying in this limbo where I suspect, but don't know. At least this way I don't have to deal with the repercussions of what his adultery would mean.

Would I leave Archer's Creek, Texas, the States? Would I take the kids and go back home to Manchester?

Home.

This is my home, it has been for over a decade. My kids are American. They've only ever visited the UK a couple of times to see my parents, and James and Dan. Their lives are here, but without Echo I know I couldn't live in this town.

My mind swirls with a cloud of what-ifs. I roll over in bed, punching my pillow in frustration at my own stupidity. I focus on falling asleep, forcing the myriad of depressing thoughts about my future to the back of my mind. My eyes fall closed, but I know sleep isn't close.

Our bedroom door opens and light from the landing spills into our darkened room. Forcing my body to still and my breathing to even, I close my eyes tightly, like the darkness can protect me from reality. This is the act I do every night. I curl my body into a protective ball away from my husband and hold my breath until he undresses and climbs into our big bed.

It used to be that the moment he got beneath the sheets he would reach for me and pull me into his arms. Distance wasn't allowed between us, not even in sleep. But now we sleep back to back, our bed so huge you could fit a truck between us.

The mattress dips and I freeze. Echo's familiar spicy, citrusy scent wafts over me and some of the tension leaves my body on a silent exhale. I expect him to roll away from me, but instead he moves across the bed until his body is nestled behind mine and his arm is across my waist.

"Livvy."

I don't know what to do. He obviously knows I'm awake. Maybe he always does and just never said anything. "Yeah," I whisper.

"Tomorrow, we need to talk, okay?"

My stomach fills with lead and tears flood my eyes. "Okay," I say, forcing the words from my dry throat.

I don't sleep at all that night and at 6am I slip from Echo's arms and creep downstairs, cautious not to wake up the kids. I fill the coffee pot, turn it on, and then stare into space, trying to quell the tide of nausea that hasn't abated since Echo told me he wanted to talk today.

My mind races through a thousand possibilities, none of them good. He's leaving me, he's cheating on me, he doesn't love me anymore. An hour later, when the kids' alarms start to go off, I'm still standing in the same spot.

Closing my eyes, I take a deep affirming breath and move. Parent mode kicks into place and I potter around the kitchen on autopilot, making lunches and placing breakfast on the table. When the kids begin to filter downstairs without being yelled at to get up, my anxiety ratchets up.

Nova walks into the kitchen in a pretty, flowered sundress.

I gawp at her. The dress is cute, age appropriate, and she looks beautiful with her hair braided into a complicated braid that falls over her shoulder. "You look beautiful," I say to her.

She blushes, rushes over, and throws her arms around my neck, hugging me. "Thanks, Mom. Tyler told me he remembered this dress last time I wore it and that I looked pretty."

"You don't just look pretty, baby, you look gorgeous."

She smiles a wide, little girl smile at me and dances over to the table to eat her breakfast.

The twins rush into the room, bouncing excitedly like only eight-year-olds can, and like every morning, they throw themselves into my waist and hold me tightly.

"Morning, Mama," they chorus.

"Morning, babies. I love you guys."

"Love you too," they say in perfect synchronicity and then push away from me and head to the table.

Zeke saunters through the door a few moments later, his hair tied back in a bun at the back of his neck. "Hey, Ma," he says, as he lowers himself into his chair at the table.

I cross the room and lift his chin with my fingers. "Wow, I'd forgotten what your face looks like. I'm loving the lack of hair curtain, but I'm sorry to say, I think the man-bun craze has finished."

Zeke rolls his eyes at me and pulls his chin from my grip. "Maybe for some, but I'm cool enough to pull it off."

Then he winks at me.

I laugh and walk to the coffee pot on the other side of the kitchen. Pulling out a mug, I pour myself a coffee, adding the hazelnut coffee creamer I'm obsessed with now, but never even knew existed when I first came to Archer's Creek.

The air in the room crackles and when I lift my eyes, Echo is standing in the doorway watching me. I look away, unable to hold his gaze, and all the happiness of a few moments before dissolves.

As if I'm on autopilot, I move mechanically through the next thirty minutes, until the kids are standing from the table and putting their bags on their shoulders. In turn, each of them says goodbye to their dad and then to me. When Zeke reaches for me and hugs me goodbye, rather than just dropping a kiss on my cheek like normal, I hold him extra tight, needing to absorb his love.

As the bus doors close, a tidal wave of anxiety washes over me. As much as I want to, I can't hide in my office to avoid my husband, so instead I turn on my heel, keeping my gaze on the floor, and scurry back into the kitchen. I can feel his eyes on me, but I refuse to acknowledge him, and busy myself cleaning up the breakfast dishes and wiping the sides down.

I know I'm being ridiculous. My husband of thirteen years wants to talk to me, and there's no reason to assume it's anything bad. But I can't force myself to believe that. Panic swells in my throat, and I can physically feel the banging of my erratic heartbeat through my chest. My body's natural fight-or-flight instinct has kicked in, and I want to run. I want to flee from this situation and protect myself from whatever he has to say.

"Livvy."

His voice makes me flinch, and like the pathetic little coward I feel, I ignore him.

"Livvy."

The sound of my name on his lips is so familiar that I almost turn and run to him out of sheer muscle memory. Instead, I pause, fighting the need to look at him.

"Olivia."

This time my name is a demand, and I spin to face him. I haven't heard that tone of voice in years. It used to be his 'don't piss me off' voice; the voice that started so many of our games and ended with me screaming out an orgasm. It's the tone I couldn't ignore if I tried, so I slowly lift my eyes until I meet his—angry, frustrated, and staring right back at me.

"Why are you ignoring me?"

"I'm not."

"Yes, you fucking are. Now what the hell is wrong with you?"

"Nothing, I'm fine. Just have loads of work to get done today," I say, lying through my teeth.

"It can wait. Do you want to go to the club for breakfast?"

"What?" I splutter. "Why?"

"Because I'm taking the day off, and you always used to love the breakfast the girls cook. Do I need a fucking reason to want to go have breakfast with my wife?"

His voice hardens, and I wince again. When did it become hard work to have a conversation with him?

"Err. No, I don't want to go. I have work to do. You go though."

Echo tilts his head to the side and assesses me. "I don't want to go on my own, I want to go with you."

"I'm busy, sorry," I say, grabbing my coffee mug and heading toward my office.

He grabs my arm as I pass, stopping me. "You're taking a day off."

I look from his hand wrapped around my arm, up to his angry green eyes. "No, I'm not," I say dismissively.

"Yes, you are. What the fuck is going on with you, Livvy?"

"You can't just tell me I'm taking the day off, Echo."

"The fuck I can't," he seethes.

Scowling at him, I try to snatch my arm from his grip, but he refuses to release me. In the blink of an eye, he bends at the waist and throws me over his shoulder.

"What the hell are you doing? Put me down." I shout, smacking at his back as he walks us up the stairs and into our bedroom. He lowers me to the floor at the foot of our bed and the moment my feet touch the ground, I push out of his grasp so quickly that I stumble backwards and land on my butt on the carpet.

Echo laughs, holding out a hand to help me up. I slap it away and struggle to pull myself upright. "You're a dick," I shout.

An amused smile appears on his face. "Get dressed. You've got fifteen minutes. If you're not ready, I'll come back up and take you back downstairs the way you got up here."

I stare at his retreating back as he turns and leaves our room. What the hell has gotten into him today? And why isn't he going to work?

I must spend longer than I thought ruminating on his behaviour, because his booming voice shouts, "Ten minutes," from the bottom of the stairs and I'm suddenly spurred into action. Whipping off my pj's, I pull out a matching bra and panties set from the dresser and slide them on. I've never been a fancy undies kind of a girl, but I draw the line at sensible cotton too, so the set is a pretty pink net and lace design that makes the most of what's left of my boobs. Despite what every baby-raising book will tell you, breastfeeding ruins your breasts. Sure, it's great for your baby and what not, but by the time you're finished baby-raising, your boobs will be heading south, empty, and seriously depressed.

I stare at myself in the full-length mirror on the back of the closet door and assess my body. Considering I've had four children, I don't look too bad. I have the usual battle scars: my stomach and thighs are crisscrossed with a million stretchmarks that have silvered over the years but are still clearly visible. My stomach hasn't been flat in a decade, and a flabby pooch remains from the twins' pregnancy, when my skin stretched so much I resembled a whale. My boobs are smaller, and my waist is thicker, but it could definitely be worse.

I'm not sexy, and I certainly don't look like the celebrities who shrink back to a perfect fucking size two a couple of hours after they give birth. I used to look at myself naked and be happy with the way I looked, now I'm indifferent. I doubt I'm alone in feeling this way; in fact I'd say most women feel similarly about their post-childbirth bodies.

Looking away from the mirror, I turn to the rail full of clothes in our closet. My style hasn't changed much in the last ten years, so I reach for a pair of denim shorts, and a black T-shirt that's been shredded across the back to make a cut-out section. I wash my face, brush my teeth, and coax my hair into a messy bun.

I give myself another quick once-over in the mirror. I look tired, and I am. The sleepless night has left me with dark circles beneath my eyes, and fear and stress is etched across my face. I could benefit from some makeup, but no amount of concealer could hide the panic in my eyes and honestly, if this conversation Echo wants to have turns out to be a bad one, then there's no point wearing mascara when it will only end up running down my face.

My feet stop working when I reach the doorway. I don't want to do this. I don't want to have this conversation, but there's no way of getting out of it now. Pulling in a deep, cleansing breath, I leave our room and make my way downstairs to my husband.

Gemma Weir

TWELVE

Echo

Scrubbing my hand down my face, I sit on the sofa and wait for Livvy to come downstairs. Things are worse than I thought. She barely wants to speak to me and obviously doesn't want to spend time with me.

How have I let things get so bad?

Life with four kids and two full-time jobs is time consuming, but I genuinely hadn't realized that Livvy and I had stopped doing anything together at all. I've normally left for work before the kids get up for school and for months I've been going to the club every night and not getting home until everyone is already in bed.

I've neglected my wife and my family. I've seriously fucked-up. I had no idea how truly bad it was until I climbed into bed with my wife last night and felt her tense at my touch. Livvy has always melted in my arms, but I barely slept last night while she held herself rigid beside me.

Pulling my cell from my pocket, I dial Anders' number.

"Echo, what's up?" Anders says when he answers.

"Hey, Boss. I need a favor."

"Name it."

"Livvy and I need some time off."

"Is everything okay?"

"Everyone's fine, but I need some time to sort some stuff out with my wife."

Anders chuckles. "Sure, no worries. Take all the time you need."

"Thanks," I say, the relief evident in my voice.

"You need Grits to take the kids?"

"No. Sleaze and Brandi are taking them to a cabin for the week."

"Okay, well shout if you need anything."

"Will do, thanks." I say, and end the call, dropping my cell back into my pocket. Everything's in place, a full week of just me and my wife.

It's time for this distance to stop.

It's time to reconnect with the woman I love.

It's time to remind my wife exactly why we're perfect together.

THIRTEEN

Libby

My heart's racing as I descend the stairs. I can hear Echo talking to someone, but his voice is too quiet for me to make out the actual conversation. I'm nervous and filled with trepidation. The urge to turn around, to run back up to our room and hide, is pulsing within me. But I don't. I steel my spine and find my big girl balls and head downstairs.

His eyes rake over me when I enter the room and I feel burned by his gaze. How can I still be so affected by him? Crossing the room, I lower myself into the chair across from the sofa and wait for him to speak.

"Let's go," he says.

"Go where?" I ask, confused. He said he wants to talk, but now he wants to go somewhere, and do what?

"Breakfast."

"I already told you I don't want to go to the club."

"Why not?" he asks, his brows twisting in confusion.

"Because I don't. I don't want to have breakfast with the club girls."

"It never bothered you in the past."

"Well, it bothers me now," I cry, feeling overwhelmed with uncertainty and apprehension. Being in a room with the women who have probably been satisfying my husband for months, is my worst nightmare.

"Livvy, what the fuck is going on with you?"

"Nothing's going on with me. Just because I don't want to go have breakfast with the club whores that crawl over you guys, shaking their pussies, and offering a blow job with every pancake eaten. It hardly seems fucking unreasonable, does it?"

Echo's jaw ticks and his mouth tightens into a firm line. "Have I ever gotten a fucking blowjob with breakfast, Olivia?"

I don't want to have this conversation, but apparently it's happening whether I like it or not. So, I tip up my chin and look him straight in the eye. "I have no idea, Echo."

His mouth falls open, like he can't believe what I just said.

"Livvy, you're starting to piss me off. You know I haven't touched a fucking club girl since before we met. What the fuck has gotten into you?"

"How would I know that, exactly?"

"How would you know what, Olivia?" Echo says, his voice

full of warning.

I hate it when he uses my full name, but we've started this conversation now, so down the rabbit hole we go. "That you haven't been getting meals with a side of slut."

Echo surges to his feet, and the sofa slides back with the force of his movements. "I have never fucking cheated on you. Why the fuck would you even suggest that? Have you cheated on me?"

"Of course not! I'd never cheat."

"Well neither would I," he roars. "Fuck, Livvy, is that what you think, that I'm fucking other women?"

Suddenly, I can't look at him. My eyes drop to my fingers twisted together in my lap.

"Livvy, fucking look at me. You think I'm cheating on you?"

I shrug, refusing to lift my gaze.

I'm aware of him moving, the air bristling around him as he gets closer. Then strong fingers grip my face tightly and my chin is lifted until I'm forced to look at him. His expression is black, and angrier than I think I've ever seen him before.

"I knew things were strained between us. But this. You think I'm fucking cheating on you? What the fuck?"

I stay silent, afraid to speak in case tears come instead.

"Hear this, Olivia, because I'm only gonna say it once and I want you to listen good and get this into your fucking head. I have never cheated on you. I haven't touched another woman or thought about touching another woman since the day I found you. Now I don't know where you got the idea into your head that I'm fucking someone else, but you need to forget that shit. Do you get me?"

Swallowing the huge lump in my throat, I look into his eyes and see nothing but truth. His fingers tighten to almost painful. "I said do you get me, Olivia?" he seethes.

I nod.

"Say it," he demands. "I need to hear you tell me you know I'm not fucking cheating on you."

"I get you," I whisper.

"Sugar, I need more than that."

"I get you. I know you're not cheating on me."

His grip on my face softens, and he strokes his thumb along the line of my jaw. "This distance between us needs to stop. Don't ever fucking doubt me again."

I nod again as the hot tears welling in my eyes spill down my cheeks.

He releases his hold on me and wipes the tears away with his fingertip. "No more tears; you crying over this bullshit is pissing me off. Get up and let's get breakfast."

I almost laugh. Only Echo would be pissed at me for crying with relief although he doesn't know that it's relief making the tears spill from my eyes. Wiping at my face, I blink back the remaining emotion that's still building and pull in a shaky inhale. *He's not cheating on me. He's not cheating on me.* I silently chant the words in my mind. I'm not sure if I'm saying the words to reassure myself or perhaps because I'm shocked that he isn't.

My heart's beating so fast I can feel it in my throat, like it's thumping so hard, it's dislodged itself and is searching for an escape. My fingers are tingling, and my legs feel numb, but the sense of relief is so overwhelming that I want to curl into a ball and sob.

My husband isn't cheating on me.

"Let's go," Echo demands, his hand held out for me to take.

I stare at it as though he were offering me a loaded gun. I don't remember the last time we held hands. With four children, there's always a small hand needing to be held, and so Echo and I just forgot how to do this.

My legs feel like lead, but I force myself to stand up and reach for his palm. This moment is insignificant in the grand scheme of things, but for some reason it feels like taking his hand is momentous. In true Echo fashion, he doesn't wait for me to reach for him. Instead, as soon as I lift my hand, he grabs mine and grips it firmly.

When our fingers are entwined, he leads me across the room and out of the front door. "I don't have shoes on," I say.

He releases my hand with a huff. "Two seconds, go."

I scurry back into the house and slide my silver sparkly converse onto my feet, then rush back out the door, pulling it closed behind me. Echo reaches for my hand again and tows me across the yard. My Escalade is parked in the driveway and

I drift toward it, but Echo marches us straight past. "What? My car's right there."

"Not taking the car. We're taking my bike."

"What?" I shriek. It's been years since I've been on his bike, and it always scared the crap out of me before.

"Don't argue, Livvy. We're taking my bike."

I fall silent, remembering the times we rode his bike together, my arms wrapped tightly around his waist, my cheek pressed against his back. When we reach the motorcycle, he drops my hand and disappears into the garage, reappearing a moment later carrying a black helmet.

"Take your hair down."

I silently acquiesce and pull the hair-tie from my hair. Echo steps close and brushes my hair out of my face, tucking it behind my ears. I hold my breath. Knowing that he hasn't betrayed our marriage is a heady feeling. I miss his touch and this closeness. I want to lean forward and kiss him, but I'm not sure he would welcome my lips. Only minutes ago, I was suggesting he was fucking other women, so it's absurd that now I want him to own my mouth like he used to in the past.

He slides the helmet onto my head and I have a flashback to the very first time he did this. I was mouthing off at him, and he threatened to spank me if I didn't behave and do as I was told. A flush of heat blooms in my stomach, but I ignore it. This isn't the time to get turned on.

Echo taps under my chin with his thumb and I immediately

tilt my face back so he can fasten the helmet straps. Once he's happy, he steps back and turns to throw his leg over his bike. He still has the same big, black, powerful motorcycle he had when we met. I'm sure he's told me what type it is at some point over the years, but I don't remember. He turns and looks at me expectantly, his jaw set into a scowl, so I take the hand he's offering me and climb on behind him.

Settling on the warm leather seat, I wrap my arms around his waist and he grabs my thighs and pulls me closer to him. I sink into the familiarity of the position and rest my cheek against his back.

The engine starts with a roar, and the edge of fear that always fills me when the bike hums beneath me flutters to life. I grip Echo tighter and feel a hand rub my leg, squeezing lightly before we start to move.

We roll down the driveway and onto the road, and when Echo twists the throttle, the bike surges forward. Even sheltered by Echo's back, the wind whips around my skin and goosebumps pebble on my arms and legs. The oh-so-familiar buzz of fear and apprehension, mixed with freedom and the feeling of flying washes over me. Closing my eyes, I relax and let myself enjoy the ride. The wind and the noise of the bike are loud, but with my eyes shut and my arms holding Echo tightly, all I hear is blissful silence. For the first time in months, my mind goes quiet and still, and I bask in the peace.

Too soon, we slow down and pull into a roadside diner,

famous for its French toast and homemade maple syrup. We've been here fairly recently with the kids, and when Echo kills the engine, I climb off the bike and pull the helmet from my head. I rest it on the seat and reach up to fluff my hair before pulling it back up into a messy bun at the top of my head.

Echo takes my hand and leads me into the diner. He guides me to an empty booth and I slide into one side while he settles on the opposite side. His eyes are solely focused on me and I fidget under his scrutiny. I glance around the diner searching for a waitress, or anything to distract myself from the conversation I know is going to happen.

A young waitress spots me and walks towards us, menus under her arm and a coffee pot in her hand. "Good morning, can I get you both some coffee?"

"Thanks," Echo says, and the young girl visibly preens. Her eyes widen, and her mouth falls into an 'O' shape when she rakes his tattooed skin with her eyes. I want to tell her he's old enough to be her father, but even in his late-forties, Echo is still an incredibly good-looking man.

She hands him a menu and fills his cup, all while flashing a seductive grin at him. Echo's expression is bored, and I almost want to laugh at her failed attempts to attract his attention.

"Is there anything else I can get you?" she asks, her voice a little breathy.

He smirks. "Yeah, how 'bout you fill my wife's coffee cup and give her a menu too?"

The girl flushes beet-red, and as if she's just remembered I'm here, she spins to face me and quickly fills my cup. She thrusts a menu into my hand without looking at me and scurries away.

When it's just Echo and I again, nerves build in my stomach and a sense of trepidation fills me. I busy myself looking at the menu. I don't know why because I always order the same thing when we come here.

A different waitress comes to take our order, and Echo orders for me before I get a chance to speak. For some reason, I'm surprised that he remembered my order, but I shouldn't be. He should know what I'd pick, just like I knew that he'd have the steak and eggs.

I hand my menu off to the waitress, and without anything else to consume my attention, I look up at the man in front of me. Echo's eyes are drilling into mine, his gaze so fierce that I feel seared.

"What the fuck is going on, Livvy?" Echo asks bluntly.

"I don't know," I reply, my voice sad and small. And it's the truth. I have no idea how we got here. I don't know how contentment became suspicion and doubt.

"I've had enough of this distance. It finishes today, now. School's out in a couple days and the kids are gonna be going with Sleaze and Brandi to the cabin they've booked."

"What," I cry, angry that he's arranged for my children to go on vacation without telling me.

"Don't fucking argue with me about this. It's happening, we need it."

"But…"

"No," Echo says, his voice low and leaving no room for argument. "The kids will have a blast; they'll be with their aunt, uncle, and cousins. I already spoke to Anders and told him that we're taking some time off."

My mouth falls open and I try to speak, but Echo cuts me off.

"You're mine, Olivia. You always have been. But it seems like you forgot that and started to doubt me and us. That's not fucking good enough. I won't ever give you up, Sugar, so it looks like I've got a week to remind you exactly who you belong to."

FOURTEEN

Echo

Livvy still hasn't said a word. I don't really care if it's good or bad silence. Right now, she's no longer in control, I am.

I'm fucking furious that she ever thought I'd touch another woman. But I know that it's my fault, I've barely been home in months and I definitely haven't been taking care of my wife the way I should.

But all that changes now.

The woman sat in front of me is my entire fucking world and I won't ever let her go. Since we had Nova, our relationship had to change and after having the rest of the kids so close together our universe revolved around diapers, onesies, and pacifiers for fucking years.

I don't regret our family—they're perfect and I fucking love them—but I hadn't realized that we'd focused so hard on being parents that we'd stopped just being *us*.

I love my wife, but I don't remember the last time I told her. I don't remember the last time we had sex; my balls are so fucking blue I swear they've shriveled up into dry, unused husks.

Fuck, we only have a week and I'm not sure that'll be enough time to bring our marriage back to life, but I sure as fuck plan to do my best to remind her exactly why we fell in love and why I own every fucking inch of her, heart, body, and soul.

The young flustered waitress from earlier brings our food, but I ignore her obvious flirtatious looks and keep all of my attention on Livvy. When the girl leaves, I watch as Livvy picks up her fork and begins to eat. I wait for the tiny of moan of pleasure I know will come the moment she slides that first piece of pancake into her mouth.

I hold my breath as she parts her lips and raises the fork, closing her mouth around it. She chews and then she moans. My cock kicks to life in my pants. That noise—so small, but so fucking sweet—just like the sound she makes when I first put my tongue on her pussy. I miss that sound. I miss her pussy, always so wet for me. My mouth waters and I try to remember the last time I tasted her, but it's been so long I can't figure out when it was.

Picking up my silverware, I eat, only taking my eyes off Livvy to glance at my plate every few moments. The food sits like lead in my gut. My anger at Livvy's unspoken accusations has morphed to fear. I could have lost her today.

Her eyes are downcast, and I take a moment to really look at my wife for the first time in months. She's beautiful. She was twenty-five when we met, but even thirteen years later she looks no different. Her hair's a mess of brown curls and her skin is tan from years of the Texan sun. She has a smattering of freckles across her nose and cheeks, and her eyes are so blue and expressive I want to fucking kick myself for not noticing she was so unhappy.

If I'd taken the time to actually look at her properly, I would have seen the doubt, the suspicion. But I didn't, and now we're sitting opposite each other, just the two of us for the first time in months and I can't think of a single fucking thing to say to the woman I love.

I shuffle around on the bench seat, poking at my food. Talking doesn't come naturally to me, not about feelings and that shit, but I need to know where her head's at. I need to know what to do to fix us.

"Why would you think I'm cheating on you?" I ask, dropping my knife and fork to my plate with a clatter.

She jumps, closing her eyes for a second and then forces her gaze up to meet mine. "Echo, I've barely seen you for months. You work all day and go to the club all night. We don't speak to each other, we don't have sex. We live in the same house, but this is the first meal we've eaten together in over six months. I know the club is always full of young, skinny, pretty girls, all more than willing to spread their legs for you. It's not exactly a leap to think you might be taking what they're offering."

I'd expected her to be vague with her answer. No idea why when Livvy has always been forthright and honest, even when the stuff she says is utter bullshit. "You know there's club stuff that I'm not allowed to tell you, Livvy, this was one of those times. Someone's been fucking with the club; that's why I've been there so much. Prez has had us in church every night for months sorting this out, running damage control. There was a rat, one of our own turned on us."

"Oh my god," she gasps. "Who was it?"

I sigh, no reason trying to keep it from her, she'll hear about it soon anyway. "Axle."

Her mouth falls open. "But Axle's a legacy; he's Anders' friend."

I nod. "I know, it's fucked up."

We both fall silent again, my mind still processing his betrayal and the fact that he fucking shot himself.

"I'm sorry."

"What for?" Livvy asks nervously.

"For not being here. I know I've been distant and haven't been around much, but I had no fucking clue you thought I was messing about on you. I'd never do that, Livvy. My cock doesn't even twitch for anyone but you. I don't want anyone but you. You're my fucking world. I'd fucking die without you."

Livvy rolls her eyes dismissively and all the pent-up anger inside of me fucking explodes. "Don't you dare fucking roll your eyes, Olivia. This is your fault too. You think I'm cheating, and you just sit there and don't say a word. I'm not fucking stupid. I know you're awake, pretending to be asleep when I get home every night. I see the way men look at you, the way they want you. You're not riding my dick, so who the fuck's sorting you out?"

Her eyes narrow and her mouth closes into a firm line. "You're a fucking asshole." She seethes. "When exactly do you think I'd get a chance to cheat? I'm either looking after the kids or working. That's it; that's all I do. I haven't been out on my own in months because you're never home to watch our kids so I can escape. Do you really want to know who's sorting me out while I'm not riding your dick as you so eloquently put it? I am. I got me a big fucking purple vibrator and I'm fucking that every night. I've got to say, right now, it's looking like a better option for a husband than you. It gives me multiple orgasms, doesn't fucking complain, and I don't have to worry about other women grinding all over it."

She falls silent for a minute, her hands clenched into tight fists. "Do you want to know why I haven't confronted you about all of this? It's because despite it all, I fucking love you. You're my fucking world too, and I'd die without you. That doesn't mean I'm not pissed at you, or that I'm happy, but it means that I wasn't ready to walk away."

"No one's walking away, Livvy. I won't fucking let you, even if you try," I tell her, my tone not leaving any room for question. "I chased you down and brought you back to me once, I'll do it again."

Something sparks in her eyes, and I watch her, unsure if it's anger or heat. Maybe she's thinking about the way I found her last time, how I bent her over the back of her friend's sofa and fucked her raw for running from me. Maybe she's thinking about how different her life would have been if I'd have left her in Manchester. But I was never going to let her leave me; she was mine then, and she's still mine now.

I push thoughts of my wife getting herself off with a dildo every night to the back of my mind. I'll think about that later, when I can decide if I'm angry that she needs a plastic cock or turned on as fuck at the idea of her fucking herself with it.

"I can't have time off work, Echo. A week without the kids isn't going to change anything and I'm too busy."

"It's done, Livvy. There's no point arguing with me. We need to spend time together, just the two of us. So, we're gonna go away for the week, somewhere with no distractions. We have to do this, so we can start to sort this shit out between us. We need time to talk, to figure out how our marriage works now, and make sure that we don't get to this point ever again."

She stares at me for a moment and then slowly nods. The tension I'd been holding onto melts away at her agreement. "I'm sorry," I say again.

"I'm sorry too," she replies.

"What are you sorry for?"

"Because you're right, this is my fault too. We both knew things were bad, but I could have said something, and I didn't. This isn't all on you. We're both guilty of neglecting our marriage. When we first got together, it was such a whirlwind. We fell in love so quickly, the attraction between us so strong, that I think we both just assumed it would last forever. But when we had the kids, our relationship changed. We couldn't play the games we used to play or argue and then fuck our issues away when we had four small children that needed us." She sighs and smiles a sad wistful smile. "We do need to figure out how our marriage works now."

I nod. "So we take the time to fix us. We talk, we fuck, and we figure out the future."

FIFTEEN

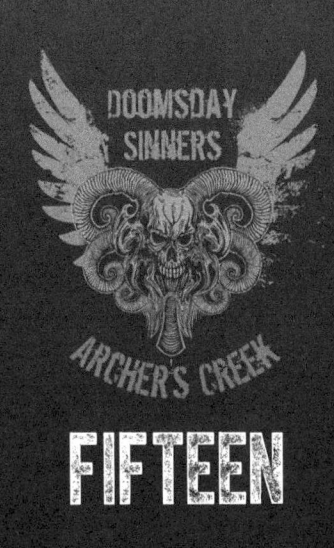

Libby

The rest of the week is a haze of work, packing, and Echo. He eats every meal with me, sleeps wrapped around me at night, and is more present in my life than he has been in years. He's kind of annoying the crap out of me.

I hadn't realised how much the kids had missed him too. The boys are vying for his attention, and Nova, his princess, is basking in his presence.

All too soon, the kids pile into the van Sleaze has rented to take his family plus our tribe, to a cabin for a week, and I tearfully hug each of my babies as they say goodbye. Echo and I stand and wave as they all drive away and despite how emotional I feel, I can't help but chuckle at how ridiculous Sleaze looks driving a van, instead of his bike or the badass truck he owns.

We watch until the van goes out of sight and then I turn to go back into the house. Echo's hand on my arm stops me. "Go get your stuff packed, we need to get going soon."

"Where are we going?"

"It's a surprise."

"Well, how am I supposed to know what to pack?"

"Livvy," Echo growls in warning.

Rolling my eyes, I turn on my heel and stomp into the house and up to our room. I pull out my overnight bag and fill it with some basics, a couple of dresses, and a bathing suit. I spot Echo's matching bag, packed and waiting next to the bed. I consider opening his bag and checking out what he's packed, but he wears the same jeans and T-shirts all year round so I doubt the contents would be illuminating. Grabbing some toiletries and stuffing them in my bag, I carry them both downstairs.

"Ready?" Echo asks when he spots me.

I nod.

He walks toward me, his stride long and purposeful. When he reaches me, he steps into my body so we're chest to chest. His palm wraps around the back of my neck and he pulls me in for a scorching kiss. His tongue parts my lips and pushes into my mouth, dominating mine and taking my lips completely. When he releases me, I'm breathless and my head is spinning with lust and heat.

"Let's go," he whispers with a knowing smirk.

Mindlessly, I let him take my hand and lead me out to his

truck. Even thirteen years later his vintage Chevy truck still makes me smile. He throws the bags into the back and opens the driver's door for me. I climb in, sliding along the warm leather bench seat and settling near the passenger door. Echo climbs in behind me slamming the door shut. He cranks the engine, puts it in gear, and backs down the driveway.

As we drive out of town, I watch the road markers, trying to figure out where he's taking me, but after twenty minutes I'm still clueless. "So where are we going?" I ask.

"Not far, about an hour."

"To a hotel?"

"Nope."

"Echo, you're being a dick; just answer the question." I snap.

His hands clench around the steering wheel and he exhales angrily, then he throws the truck sideways and we skid to a stop on the side of the road. "What the fuck?" I cry, shoving at his shoulder.

Grabbing my hands, he holds them still. "Olivia, I wasn't gonna say anything about this yet, but I think it's fucking time. I figured out what's changed about our marriage. It's that I stopped being the one in control. When we first got together, I was in charge and you fucking loved that—you fought me and we both loved that too. We played our games, and that's what kept the balance in our relationship. The last few years we've stopped doing it, we stopped playing, and that's when we started to drift apart. This week that changes. I'm taking back the power in our marriage, starting right fucking now; so sit back, shut the fuck up, and you'll find out where we're going when we get there."

He doesn't wait for my response; he drops my hands and turns the truck back onto the highway. Words grow and then die in my mouth. He's right, our push and pull games where he demanded and I refused, were a big part of our relationship for years. I don't know why we stopped playing with each other; perhaps it was because we were both exhausted from working and looking after our family, and all we wanted was a good night's sleep? Or maybe it was that becoming parents made us feel like we had to grow up and stop playing games all together?

Leaning back in the seat, I try to remember when we started to drift apart. I can't pinpoint it down to an exact day, just that instead of my stomach trembling with anticipation every time he came near me, I just started to accept it as normal. I never stopped being attracted to Echo. He's an incredibly good-looking man, and although his six pack isn't as defined as it used to be, he's still fit and muscled.

Until the last year we still had sex, but instead of the passionate marathon sessions we used to have, we got good at knowing how to get each other off to get to the goal quicker.

Loving Echo is the easiest thing I've ever done, and I can't imagine ever not loving him. But I think we need to fall back in love with each other and maybe this is the way to do that.

Neither of us speaks for a long while. The radio's playing quietly, but the truck's cab still feels incredibly small and uncomfortable when it's filled with this much tension.

"Come here," Echo says, his voice low.

It's unmistakably an order and a frisson of fear mixes with excitement. I slide along the seat and he pulls me closer until our thighs are pressed side by side and his arm is draped over my shoulders.

"I forgot how much it turns me on when you do what I tell you."

"I forgot how much I like you telling me what to do." I admit quietly.

We fall silent again, but instead of the tension between us being angry, now it feels charged. I know there's going to be sex involved this week: hot, angry, cathartic sex. I need Echo to fuck me and I can't wait, but it's not just about the physical contact. We need to talk, to reconnect and remember why we love each other so much.

He's right, we need this time.

Forty minutes later, we turn off the highway and drive through a town called Anatera. It's not unlike Archer's Creek, with a row of shop fronts and restaurants on either side of a town square, along with a bandstand and park benches.

We pull into a parking space outside a hardware shop and I turn to look at Echo in confusion.

"Stay here, Sugar, I'll be right back."

I nod and watch as he climbs out the truck and strides into the store. A few moments later he walks back out and climbs into the truck.

"Here," he says, handing me a key.

Pulling away from the curb, we drive for another ten minutes and then pull off the main road and head down a bumpy dirt track. I twist my head from side to side, looking for a signpost or any kind of indication of where we're going, and then a minute later I see it. A beautiful wood cabin comes into view, its single storey, a mix of traditional logs and uber modern glass walls and sleek lines. It's gorgeous.

"Is this where we're staying?"

Echo smiles at the obvious enthusiasm in my voice. "Yep, this place is ours for the next week."

"It's beautiful," I gush. "How did you find out about this place?"

"Lord. He knows the guys who owns them. There are two more hidden out in the woods too."

We slow to a stop, and I spring out of the truck and head to the front door, the key gripped tightly in my hand. I know I should probably wait for Echo, but I'm too eager to get inside, so I push the key into the lock and open the door.

The cabin's open plan, light and airy, with a huge log fire, a comfy looking sofa, and a modern kitchen. The bedroom door is partially open, and a massive sleigh bed seems to dominate the space. I walk towards the room and push the door open the rest of the way. The room is made up of two walls of glass that make the space feel like it's part of the surrounding wilderness. A large black control panel catches my eye and I cross the room to it. A label above one of the switches says *windows* and curious, I press it. The glass instantly turns smoky, obscuring the view. I laugh and press the button again and the smoke disappears, and the windows clear.

"You having fun?" Echo drawls from the doorway.

I turn to him, a broad smile on my face. "Yes, this place is amazing."

Echo twists to take in the rest of the room. "That's one hell of a tub."

I follow his gaze and my eyes land on the biggest copper tub I've ever seen in my life, right there in the middle of the bedroom. "Holy crap, I hadn't even noticed that." A smoked glass screen hides the toilet, sink, and shower beyond it.

Moving past Echo, I head into the kitchen, admiring the wooden butcher block counters and huge oven. Doors at the back of the cabin pull my attention and I push on the handle, only to find that the door easily folds then concertinas into the next, until the entire back of the cabin is open.

A deck wraps around the back of the house, with a huge hot tub situated in the corner. Leaning my elbows on the deck railing, I look out onto the beautiful meadow surrounding us. Trees frame the house, becoming denser at the end of the open space. It's quiet, peaceful, and perfect.

Echo's body presses against mine, his elbows resting on either side of mine on the railing. I can feel the heat of his skin through my T-shirt, and I close my eyes as need and want flow through me.

"You like?" he asks.

"It's beautiful."

"I'm glad."

"Lift your arms into the air," he rasps into my ear.

"What?" I say, turning to look at him.

"You heard me, Livvy. Lift your hands into the air."

"Echo?"

"I told you I was taking back control of our relationship, well that starts now. Don't you remember how this works, Sugar? We both like it when you do as you're told."

A shudder runs through me and my eyes fall closed. I remember his voice when it's all low and raspy like this and heat pools between my legs. Slowly, I release my grip on the railing and lift my arms into the air.

"That's it, Sugar, you do remember," he says as he lifts the hem of my shirt, taking his time, before pulling it over my head and dropping it to the floor.

He unclasps my bra and I lower my arms, so he can slide that off too. Cool air wafts across my exposed nipples making them harden, and I fight the urge to cover myself. No one can see us out here in the middle of nowhere, so I drop my arms to my sides.

"Hold onto the rail."

I immediately grip the rail tightly and his lips press to the back of my neck. I curl into his touch, the heat of his lips warming my skin. His hand slides around my ribs and cups one of my breasts. I watch his movements, gasping when he rolls my nipple between his thumb and forefinger. Back and forth he rolls, gradually increasing the pressure, until the pain is almost greater than the pleasure.

I cry out and he squeezes tighter then releases. The pulse of wonderful pain makes my knees buckle and my chin drop. I groan loudly and feel Echo's dark chuckle rumble behind me.

"You always did enjoy a bit of pain with your pleasure."

I nod, unable to speak, but feeling like I need to respond. His hands drop to my shorts and he quickly unbuttons them and pushes them down to the floor.

"Step out," he orders, and I comply, watching as he kicks them out of the way.

"Shoes off."

I quickly kick them off, flicking them across the decking, not caring where they land.

"Spread your legs."

I widen my stance, impatiently waiting for him to touch me, but nothing happens. I look over my shoulder and find him staring at me.

"Echo," I whine, needy and impatient.

"What's up, Sugar?"

"What are you doing? Touch me."

"I'm enjoying the view."

"Echo," I snap.

A second later the heavy weight of his body lands on my back. He pushes me forward until my stomach is resting on the railing and I'm bent over it. He unceremoniously kicks my legs wider apart and pushes his hard cock against my ass. "You don't get to call the shots here, Livvy. I do. If I want to stand and fucking stare at your ass for an hour, I will, and you'll do as you're told because the only way I'll fuck you is if you're behaving. Do you understand?"

"Oh, Jesus, I remember this game," I purr breathily.

"So do I. You used to fucking love it. Do you now? I bet if I touched your pussy you'd be soaking wet, wouldn't you?"

"Why don't you touch me and find out?" I taunt, falling so easily back into the role of defiant.

He licks a path up the back of my neck with his tongue and grinds his cock against me again. "The problem is Livvy, that your pussy hasn't been mine in far too long. You've been sharing it."

"What?" I cry, confused.

"What was it you said? Oh, I remember. You said that you'd gotten yourself a big fucking purple vibrator, and that you were fucking that every night."

"Oh shit," I hiss, needing him to touch me, but unsure what the hell he's going to do now. This was why I loved our games; the intensity, the fear of the unknown, but knowing that everything he did to me was fucking unbelievable and guaranteed to end with me screaming out in orgasm.

"Don't move," he orders and his weight lifts from my back.

I want to squirm and move, but I manage not to. I stay bent over the railing, naked except for my lace boy shorts and wait. Butterflies flutter in my stomach. I'm nervous, but happy, excited, and eager for him to come back. I want to feel his hard cock inside of me; God, I need him to make me come. I can give myself an orgasm easily, but it's so much better when it's him: his fingers, his tongue, just him.

The sound of his returning footsteps is loud, and the butterflies in my stomach stop fluttering and start to do sprints. My heart beats quicker and I twist my head, needing to see him to quell the rising tide of excited nerves. In this position I know he's behind me, but I can't see him. The urge to turn and look for him battles with my inbuilt desire to obey his command not to move.

Closing my eyes, I drop my head and wait. He obviously plans to torture me, but I can play this game. Right now, I want him more than I want to defy him. A noise breaks the silent peace of the cabin and I instantly tense. The sound is familiar—a low whirring noise—and I know… I know what it is, and my core pulses.

Twisting my head, I find Echo now standing a few steps behind me. His hands are behind his back, and his eyes are hooded and intense. I watch him rake my mostly naked form with his eyes, and when his gaze moves back to my face, our eyes lock, and he smirks. I swear time slows down as he brings his hands from behind his back and there gripped in his palm is my big, purple vibrator, buzzing away. "Oh shit."

His laugh is cold and distant. "Open your mouth, Livvy."

I drop my chin to my chest and close my eyes. I should have known the moment I told him about my vibrator he would lose his shit over it. But fuck him, I bought that thing because he wasn't around; he can't be mad at me for that.

I feel the vibration as he skims the plastic along my cheek. "Open up, Livvy. You're gonna want this nice and wet."

Compelled to comply, I open my eyes, turn my face, and open my mouth. He slides the vibrator along my tongue until two or three inches are inside my mouth and the low vibration hums along my flesh.

"Suck," he orders. "I want to watch you."

I close my mouth around the plastic and suck, running my tongue up and down the length, coating it in saliva. He pushes it further into my mouth, then pulls it out until just an inch is left inside. "How does it taste, Livvy? Is plastic cock as good as my dick?"

I shake my head but open my mouth and swirl my tongue around the tip of the vibe just to piss him off. His eyes darken, and he lifts one of my hands from the railing and wraps it around the base of the toy.

"Suck it. Show me how satisfying it is to give your toy a blow job."

I exaggeratedly run my tongue over the toy and then pull it from my mouth. "That's the thing about plastic dicks; they don't need any foreplay, they're always ready to go."

His lips twitch into a smile and he takes the vibe from me and pushes my hand back to the railing. He turns the vibrations up on the toy and runs it straight down between my ass cheeks. I jump, and he pulls the toy away, then does it again, dipping the tip lower each time until he reaches my sex.

My panties are soaking wet, and I shift my weight from leg to leg, trying to push him closer to my pussy. The vibrator glances across my clit, then it's gone. Instead, Echo pushes it lightly against my asshole. I mewl, bowing away from the sensation, then immediately push back into it, loving the feeling, but hating that my panties are a barrier. He's doing this deliberately, torturing me and teasing me. Part of me is loving this, the build-up and foreplay; but the needy, hot, frustrated part of me wants to spin around, take the vibrator from him and go sort myself out.

"Echo." I gasp, when he slides the vibe along my sex, pressing against my opening before teasing my clit and then pulling away.

"What's up, Sugar?"

"I need you to touch me."

"I thought a plastic cock was a better husband than me? Less hassle?"

"Stop. I get it, but you can't be mad at me for getting myself off when you weren't there to do it." I cry.

"Oh, I'm not mad. I'm fucking furious, Livvy. But not just at you. I'm mad at me too. I'm fucking furious that my woman had to buy a sex toy to keep herself satisfied because I wasn't taking care of her." His voice is angry and gruff, and the vibe is still between my legs buzzing away but not offering me any satisfaction. His other hand slides along my back, down my ass cheeks and he roughly shoves my panties down.

Echo pushes the toy into my pussy in one long thrust. I cry out, loving the feeling of fullness as he pushes the toy further into my dripping wet sex and holds it still. The vibrations make my sex muscles clench, and I try to roll my hips to create friction.

"This cunt is mine. I claimed it when I first met you and I'm gonna show you exactly who owns it again this week. But first I want you to show me how good this toy gets you off. If this is my competition, I want to watch you ride this dildo and make yourself come."

I rise onto my tiptoes, allowing the toy to slide almost all the way out of my pussy, then slowly sink back down, rolling my hips and making the toy hit my G-spot. I groan once it's fully seated inside of me, pausing for a second to enjoy the pulsing vibration. I rise again and the toy slides out, but this time I sink back down onto it quicker. Echo's holding the vibe with one hand, but he uses the other to spread my ass cheeks and I know he's watching the toy slide in and out of me.

"You're so wet, Livvy. My hand's soaked. Is it the toy that's making you cream this much, or is it that I'm holding it while you fuck it? That I'm watching your pussy swallow it?"

I lift up and sink back down. Again and again, I ride the toy, wishing I could reach for my clit and bring myself to orgasm. But I don't. This is all part of the game. Echo wants to control this, to control me, and he told me to keep my hands on the railing, so I don't move. Lifting up, I drop down onto the toy harder, chasing my orgasm and wishing it was Echo's cock and not a toy that I was fucking.

"Do you fuck your ass with this toy too?" he asks, his voice low.

"No," I rasp out, as I sink back down and the toy hits my G-spot again, making my eyes roll.

"Why not? You used to love my cock deep in your ass, fucking you until you were writhing and screaming."

I rise up and down quicker now, riding the toy with earnest. So wet and turned on that I know I'm getting close to release.

"Why not?" Echo demands.

"Because I have a butt plug, and I use that instead," I cry.

I rise up, but the toy is pulled free of my pussy and when I sink down it's gone. "What the fuck?" I scream, twisting my neck to look at Echo.

"You want this, Sugar?" he asks, lifting the toy up and showing me how wet it is.

I nod quickly, twisting my hips, unable to stay still. A moment later he pushes the toy back into my sex again, and

I moan loudly in pleasure. I start to ride, harder and faster, desperately pushing myself closer to release, in case Echo decides to take the toy away again.

"Did you plug your ass and then fuck yourself with this dildo, Livvy?" he asks, his other hand gripping my ass cheek hard.

"Yes," I gasp, so close to release I can feel the sensation building in my stomach.

"How did it feel, to have both your holes filled at the same time?"

"So fucking good," I scream, as my orgasm takes hold and I tense around the toy, shuddering and shivering as my pleasure overwhelms me. As my orgasm subsides, I slump over the railings, my muscles unable to hold me any longer and I feel the toy slide from my pussy.

I make a pitiful, keening moan, my body suddenly empty, and I try to squeeze my thighs together to prolong the blissful feeling of fullness I'd felt only moments before.

"How do you feel, Sugar?" Echo asks, his wet hand sliding up my side as he crowds me with his body.

"Good." I purr softly.

He chuckles brokenly. "Is it better than my cock?"

My muscles are lax, but I slowly turn my face to look at him and shake my head. "No."

"Do you remember what it's like to have your cunt stuffed full of my hard cock?"

I shake my head again.

"Would you rather have a plastic dildo or me?" he demands.

Our gazes lock and for a moment I swear I can see a hint of insecurity in his eyes. He blinks and it's gone, and all that's left is a dominant gleam that I remember, but haven't seen in a very long time.

Butterflies burst to life in my stomach. "You," I say huskily.

His hands fall to his waist and he slowly undoes his jeans, lowering the zipper until his hard cock bobs free. My mouth waters at the sight of it. Hard and thick and long. I can't decide whether I want him in my mouth or my pussy more, but I know that I need him, anyway I can get him. "I forgot what your cock looks like," I taunt.

"You need an up-close reminder, Sugar?"

"I forgot what it feels like too," I challenge.

He chuckles, and the low sound has goosebumps pebbling across my heated skin. "Then maybe it's time to remind you. I'm gonna fuck you until you remember exactly what it feels like to have a real cock inside your cunt."

He steps up behind me and both of his hands land on my ass cheeks. I feel his fingers caress the skin until he grips firmly and spreads my cheeks. His hard dick probes at my entrance, barely dipping into my sex before pulling back. He's teasing me, torturing me and punishing me, and I want him more than I've wanted anything in as long as I can remember.

He pushes just the head inside and then withdraws

completely. An agonised growl forms in my throat and I wait for him, shaking with need. I'm desperate, poised to thrust back against him and force him all the way into me. Before I have a chance to take him, he slams all the way into my cunt in one long, hard thrust, and I scream.

The raw guttural sound flows from my mouth without my volition and I lurch forward, my stomach slamming into the railing I'm resting on. Before I can adjust to his size, he pulls out and slams back into me. His cock is so much bigger than my vibrator, and my pussy struggles to accommodate him.

Echo doesn't allow me any time to compose myself before he begins to fuck me at a frantic pace. His balls slap against my ass as he thrusts in and out of me, and all I can do is hold onto the railing and ride out the storm as Echo takes ownership of me.

"Remember now, Livvy? Do you remember what it feels like when I fuck you until you give yourself over to me completely?"

I open my mouth to speak, but before I can form words, he pulls his cock from my pussy, drops to his knees, and slams his mouth against my sex. His tongue fucks me while his fingers pinch and rub at my clit. My knees go weak, but I lock them, keeping myself upright by sheer will.

An orgasm bursts to life, but before it can ignite, his tongue is gone, and his cock is filling me again. This time his pace is excruciatingly slow and deep. I feel every ridge of his cock as he drags it in and out of my swollen sex.

His fingers tangle into my hair and a sharp burst of pain tingles across my scalp, as he drags my head until my back arches, and he pushes even deeper inside, filling me completely.

"Do you feel that, Sugar? You're so full of my dick, all you can do is moan and pant. I fucking own this cunt; it belongs to me, and for the next week I'm gonna take you again and again until nothing will ever compare. I'm gonna own every fucking gasp, every fucking sigh, every fucking pant. It's all mine, you're all mine."

I'm mindless, unable to form coherent thoughts, my entire world revolves around the push and pull of his dick. I can feel my orgasm swirling and building, but I need him to make me plunge over the edge.

He slides his cock almost all of the way out, and stills. I try to move, but with my hair still held in his grip and my back curved, I'm completely at his mercy, ruled by his whims.

"Do you want me to make you come?" he asks, his voice rough and low.

I try to nod, but only manage to twitch against his hold. With a hard slam, he sinks all the way back inside of me and I jerk forward with the force. A shrill cry falls from my lips and my eyes roll when a wave of pleasure engulfs me.

Slowly he slides out and then slams back in. A crescendo of ecstasy detonates within me and I scream as the most intense orgasm I think I've ever felt overtakes me.

Fresh waves of bliss hit me with each move of his dick, and

moments later I feel him swell impossibly large and the heat of his release scorches my sex as he comes.

I don't know how long we stay connected; his sweaty chest against my back, my stomach slumped over the railing, and his softening dick still inside of me. His arm is now wrapped around my stomach preventing me from collapsing, and I haven't felt this drunk on pleasure in years. My eyes are still closed but I'm smiling, and happy tears are rolling down my cheeks.

This is what I've missed. This is what I needed. Echo mastered my body and took control of my pleasure and I'm exhausted—sticky with a mixture of sweat, his cum, and my own arousal. But I couldn't care less, because I feel light and free, and loved and wanted, and I had no idea how much I'd craved that until this very moment.

"I think someone needs a nap." Echo says against my ear.

I nod, my eyes still closed. Echo's weight lifts from me and he scoops me into the air, one arm around my back, the other beneath my legs. Lethargy has consumed me, and I snuggle into his warm, familiar chest and let him carry me.

I don't open my eyes until I feel the soft comforter beneath my back. He lowers me into the bed and pulls the sheets up to cover me. "Sleep, Sugar. I'm gonna go into town and get us some dinner."

I'm too happy, sated, and sleepy to argue, so I snuggle deeper into the bed and close my eyes. Echo's soft chuckle is the last thing I remember before I fall asleep.

SIXTEEN

Echo

Closing the door to my truck, I drop my head to the steering wheel and close my eyes. I'm a fucking idiot. How the fuck did I forget how perfect my wife is when she comes? I just watched her get herself off on a vibrator. I'm jealous of a plastic fucking dildo, and I've been missing out on my wife's pussy for nearly a year. What the hell is wrong with me?

I hadn't planned to fuck her with it. I'd planned to tease her with the toy and then smash it into a million pieces so she could never use it again. But then she'd gotten so fucking wet and I couldn't resist watching her pussy slide up and down it. Jesus, when she said she had a butt plug that she uses as well, I almost came in my jeans like a fucking teenager.

I'd found the toy in her dresser drawer. It hadn't been

hidden, but now I wish I'd dug around a bit deeper, because fuck knows what else she had in there. God, my cock is hard again just thinking about what she'd look like with a plug filling up her ass, stretching her tight hole out for me.

Fucking Livvy had been like coming home and realizing you live in a perfect nirvana. She's heaven and hell to me. Her cunt's so wet, hot, and tight that I want to stay with my cock buried in her all day every day. But once I'm inside her, my inner fucking caveman beats at my chest and I'm consumed with thoughts of branding her and owning her and filling her with my cum.

I want her again already and I was balls deep inside her less than twenty minutes ago. I've missed out on too much time with her like this because we forgot to look after our relationship. There's a knot wound so tightly inside my chest, taunting me that I could lose her. That she could walk away from me, because she's not as tightly connected to me now, as she was all those years ago when we found each other.

I should have made love to her, not fucked her over the decking rail, but I just couldn't help myself. I should have shown her how much I love her, how much I need her, but once she was naked all I could think about was showing her I owned her, that she's still mine.

We have a week here together. Seven days for me to remind her that she belongs to me, that we only work when we're connected and in tune. I need to control her, and she needs to fight that control. The desire to overpower her and dominate her has never gone away, but over the years it's diluted because I took for granted that she was mine forever.

Her unhappiness, her doubt, is a fucking slap in the face, and a wake-up call that I won't ignore. By the time we go home, my wife's going to be well fucked, well loved, and mine again.

Filled with resolve, I start the truck and make my way back into town. Stopping at the store, I grab a few groceries, then head to a little Italian place to get takeout for dinner. The host on the counter takes my order, and once I've paid I turn away from the desk and move toward a bench, set up on the far wall. Something catches my eye through the window of the restaurant and I pause, then take a step closer to the window to look out. Opposite the restaurant is a small side street and halfway down is a doorway with a red sign above it.

I scoff to myself. What are the fucking chances that in a small town like Anatera there would be a sex toy store? But there it is. Chuckling to myself, I push open the restaurant door and quickly cross the road. The sign above the store proudly boasts that 'The Pleasure Dome' sells the finest sex toys, lingerie, and fetish gear.

Pushing open the door, I enter the shop and a twenty-something woman smiles at me.

"Hey there. Feel free to look around and just give me a shout if you can't find what you need."

I nod, but don't speak. Slowly, I make my way around

the store, looking at the vast array of dildos, vibrators, nipple clamps, and butt plugs, as well as a whole host of freaky looking contraptions that I have no idea what you do with.

I pause in front of the butt plugs. I can't get the idea out of my head, and before I know what I'm doing, I'm lifting a metal plug from the shelf and looking at the pink jewel that's sunk into the top of it. My cock kicks in my pants again and I silently groan.

I've never really messed about with sex toys before. I'm more than capable of making a woman come without any help. But now Livvy's planted the idea of her ass being filled with a plug, I can't stop thinking about it. The plug comes in two different sizes, so I grab the smaller of the two and a bottle of lube and take them to the counter. The woman rings up my purchases and slides them into a black plastic bag. I pay, thank her, and leave the store.

My cock's rock hard, but I'm not gonna be the creepy fucker groping at his cock as he comes out of a sex store, so I will my boner to settle down, and head back to the restaurant to pick up my takeout.

The drive back to the cabin seems to take forever, and when the log house comes into view, I can't help glancing at the bag full of goodies next to me. An image of Livvy spreading her cheeks to show me the plug flashes into my mind and my cock jerks to life. Killing the engine, I lift the bag from beside me and open the door. Our duffels are still in the bed of the truck, so I grab them both in one hand and lift them out. Walking around to the passenger door, I open it and reach for the sex store bag, sliding it inside my duffel and adjusting my rock hard dick before I grab the takeout and head into the cabin.

Opening the door, I scan the open space and see that the living room is quiet and empty. I kick the door shut behind me and cross to the kitchen, placing the takeout on the counter. The door to the bedroom is half open, and I can just see the outline of Livvy beneath the sheets of the huge bed. Smiling to myself, a flush of pure male pride fills me. My wife is napping because I gave her enough orgasms to exhaust her.

Not wanting to wake her, I place our duffels on the floor and head back out to my truck to retrieve the groceries. I try to be as quiet as possible as I empty the food into the fridge and put the takeout in the oven to keep warm.

Almost on instinct, I turn to look into the bedroom. I should wake her up so she can eat, but the lure of her naked body beneath the sheets is more temptation than I can resist. I cross the room in six long strides and I'm through the door and standing beside the bed. She's buried beneath the comforter, with only her face visible. Her hair is sex tousled and messy from my hands, and although I can't see any of her skin, I can imagine the way she looks: naked, sated, and asleep.

Dragging the collar of my shirt up, I pull it over my head, discarding it onto the floor. My jeans and boots quickly follow and then I lift the comforter and climb into bed behind her.

I want to pull her into my chest, but the memory of her flinching from my touch has me questioning if she'd welcome my arms around her. I freeze next to her, my body not touching hers as I try to decide what to do.

"Echo?" she says sleepily.

"Yeah, Sugar?"

"Hey," she says, crawling into my chest and resting her head in the nook between my neck and shoulder.

I exhale a relief filled breath. I don't remember the last time she lay curled into my chest like this, and I feel like an even bigger fucking idiot for not noticing that we'd fallen so far apart. From the moment I first met her, I've always wanted—no, *needed*—her close to me. There was no room for distance between us when she was always in my arms.

But it wasn't easy to hold her when there were four babies who all wanted her closeness as well. Lying here now, I know I should have fought harder, held her while she held the kids, rather than standing back and allowing distance to become our normal.

"Did you get dinner? I'm starving," she asks and roots further into my body, her leg brushing up against mine.

"Yeah, it's in the oven, keeping warm."

She nods against my chest and then her fingers wander across my skin. The movements feel absentminded, but then her fingers seem to find purpose. She explores my chest and abs, moving over the ridges of my pecs, and in and out of the hollows of my abs. I hold my breath so I don't disturb her. Everywhere her fingers touch my skin feels scorched. I want her hands on me, I want her to reacquaint herself with the way my body feels beneath hers. I want her to claim me, to own me with the same intensity that she used to.

My lungs stop working when her fingers dip lower, running along the edge of my boxers.

"Can I touch?" she asks, and I hate that I can hear the uncertainty in her voice.

"I'm yours, Sugar. You don't need to ask."

I hold my breath as she remains unmoving for a second, and then her small hand slides beneath the fabric of my boxers. My body is a mass of reaction as my lungs kick-start again and my heart beats wildly, uncontrollably. Her probing fingers sink lower, running from the tip of my cock all the way to my heavy, aching balls. "Fuck," I rasp.

She lifts her head from my chest and looks at me. "Do you want my hand or my mouth?"

"Whichever you want, Sugar." I force out, trying to hide the way my voice cracks with desperation.

Her blue eyes flick up to me and I can see the mischief in them. "I thought you were in control this week?"

She's playing with me. I don't know why I'm so relieved by her mocking words, but a pressure lifts from my chest and I smile, the biggest smile I've had in months. "Well hell, Sugar; you're right. Is that what you want? Do you want my dick in your mouth, or would you rather I go get your dildo and you can give me a show with that instead?"

"No, I want you."

"Tell me."

"I want your dick in my mouth. I want to suck you and lick you and taste you."

"That's right, Sugar, 'cause that mouth belongs to me doesn't it?"

Livvy smirks, but nods solemnly.

Chuckling, I grab my hard length. "Get your mouth around my cock. I want to watch you take it all."

She grins, and it's wide and joyful, then she throws back the comforter, making the bed bounce as she excitedly shimmies towards my twitching eager dick.

"Oh, and Livvy…" I say.

Pausing, she looks up at me, her eyes filled with humor.

"I expect you to swallow every drop."

Her pink tongue dips out and I watch as she licks her lips. Her eyes go hooded as she regards my hard cock and she looks at my length, then to me and smirks. She leans forward and swallows me whole, and my hips buck, and my eyes roll back in my head. A growl like moan escapes from my throat and I swear I nearly blow against her tongue just from that first feel of her hot little mouth.

Lapping at the underneath of my cock with her tongue, she sucks up and down my dick, her other hand cupping my balls and squeezing them lightly. My wife gives amazing head, and it's taking all I have not to come.

I try to close my eyes, but I don't want to miss a moment of the way she looks, her mouth stretched around my dick. She's between my legs on her knees, her head bent over my cock, her ass in the air, moving up and down as she devours me.

I wish there was a mirror at the end of the bed, so I could watch her tight ass sway. My mind goes to the plug in my duffel, and I swear I get harder at the thought of her giving me head, bent over with that pink sparkly plug firmly sat in her ass.

My hand moves to her head and I bury my fingers in her curls and tug. She moans around my dick, and if I could reach her, I'd lay money on her cunt being wet again. She sucks harder, swirling her tongue around the tip and my resolve shatters. I'm gonna come. I feel it start to rise in my gut and gripping her hair tighter, I hold her head down so my dick hits the back of her throat. She hums, and the vibration is my undoing. I come, filling her mouth with spurt after spurt of my seed.

My gaze is fixated on her and I watch as she swallows every drop of my release, licking the remnants from my cock until she slowly lifts her head up, releasing my dick with a pop. Our eyes lock and knowing I'm watching, her tongue dips out, and she licks her lips like she can't get enough of the taste of me.

"Fuck."

Livvy smiles, leans over, and places a light kiss against the tip of my cock then she slides off the bed and sashays out of the room completely naked.

Groaning, I drop my head back to the pillow and let my eyes fall closed. My breathing is ragged and my cock's still twitching, eager to get started on round two. I can hear Livvy moving around in the kitchen and only the thought of her prancing about naked is enough to pull me from the bed.

I don't bother to dress. Instead I follow my wife, naked, with my semi-hard cock leading the way. My stride is fast and eager, until my eyes land on her naked ass, then I slow my pace and enjoy every moment of watching Livvy prancing about the kitchen with nothing on.

The smell of rich garlic and cream hits my nose and my stomach rumbles on cue. Livvy throws a smile over her shoulder to me then pushes up onto her tiptoes to reach two plates from the cupboard in front of her.

We eat side by side, naked, at the built-in bar in the kitchen. The food is amazing and so is the view. I feel like a fucking teenager. I keep stealing glances at her nipples: perky and on display, and close enough I could lean forward and take one into my mouth. Her body's changed as she's gotten older, developed and matured, and she's still as sexy to me as ever. I don't know how she feels about the way she looks—I've never taken the time to ask her—but I already want to drag her back to the bedroom and worship every fucking perfect inch of her.

"Wow, that was great," she says, patting at her stomach and pushing her plate away.

My fingers are twitching with the desire to pull her into my lap and slide my dick into her perfect pussy again. But as much as this week is about us reconnecting physically, it's about more than that. We've fallen out of the habit of talking to one another. Sure, we talk about the kids, but we don't talk about us anymore.

I rise from my seat and load both of our plates and silverware into the dishwasher, then I walk around the kitchen island and stand in front of Livvy. "Come sit with me," I say, holding out my hand for her to take.

She smiles and lifts her hand, placing it in mine. My heart thumps in my chest just from the innocent touch of her fingers against my palm. Two days ago, I had to physically take her hand; she wouldn't give it willingly. It might seem like a thoughtless action—and it probably was—but I need her to give herself to me, I always have. I lead her across the room to the huge sofa and sink down into it, pulling her with me and into my lap. "I love you in my lap," I say, nuzzling my nose into her neck and inhaling her scent. She smells sweetly of the apple bodywash she uses, and of me.

"I love you," I say, needing to tell her the words, to remind her she's my everything.

Her body melts into mine and she rests her head against my chest. "I love you too. Some days I wish I didn't, but I do. I love you so much."

"We'll get things sorted between us, Sugar. You're my world, and I'll fight to put us back together again."

She nods, and I feel the movement rather than see it.

"I miss you," she whispers.

The words are like a knife in the heart. Pulling her across me, I move her until she's straddling my lap, her legs on either side of me. "Why didn't you say anything?"

She shrugs. "I didn't even realise it was happening until it got to a point when I didn't remember the last time we touched or spoke about something other than the kids."

"Fuck, Livvy, we need to do better, try harder. Both of us, because I won't ever let you go. Talk to me, let's talk about all of the shit we forgot to tell each other."

She laughs. "Like what?"

"I don't know, everything. Tell me about your week, tell me about a show you're watching, a book you're reading. Fuck, I don't care, tell me all the latest gossip Brandi told you."

She giggles and then we start to talk.

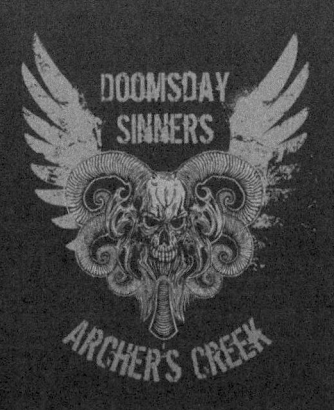

SEVENTEEN

Libby

I don't remember the last time Echo and I sat down and just spoke to one another like this. I'm still straddling his lap and pretending that I don't feel his hard cock pressed up against my sex, because I'm enjoying having a random, meaningless conversation with my husband.

"I've gotten a bit obsessed with these supernatural shows. You know, the ones with angels and demons and vampires. They're like car crash T.V. but once I start I can't stop, and I swear I watched like five episodes back-to-back the other day."

Echo chuckles, his hands on my thighs, his thumb drawing circles on my bare skin. "I don't remember the last time I even turned the T.V. on. All this shit at the club has been playing on my mind and by the time I've gotten home, all I want to do is go to sleep and forget about all the crap I've had to deal with that day."

Guilt hits me like a bullet. Echo's been dealing with a member of the club betraying them. To the outside world someone turning on you would piss you off, maybe upset you, but it wouldn't be the end of the world. But to an MC, when you become a member you do it for life. It's a brotherhood, a family, and loyalty is everything to them. For one of their brothers to betray them, they must be devastated.

"How did Anders take everything that's happened with Axle? They were close, weren't they?"

Echo sighs, lifting one of his hands from my leg and rubbing it wearily across his eyes. "Yeah, they were close. Both of them were legacy, been friends since Anders moved to town. Prez is pretty cut up, he offered us all a get-out clause."

"What?" I say, shocked.

"Yep, at church the other night. He told us if any of us wanted out we could turn in our cut then and there and leave; no retribution."

"Wow. Did you consider it?"

"Would you have wanted me to?"

"I don't know. It's not something I've ever really thought about. You were a part of the club long before I met you, and I've never considered you not being a Sinner. It's who you are."

"I can't imagine life without the club, my brothers."

I think about what our lives would look like without our

friends and family at the Sinners, and I just can't picture it. Our entire story would be different if Echo wasn't a Sinner. In fact, we probably wouldn't have lasted past our first meeting on the side of the road all those years ago.

"They're our family," I say, and truly mean it.

Echo exhales, and I hadn't realised he'd been holding his breath, waiting for me to speak. "I'm a Sinner until my last breath, Livvy. You're right; it's who I am."

"I know," I say, leaning forward and placing a kiss against his lips.

We spend the rest of the night talking, and he tells me what he can about Axle. I know he isn't telling me everything, but over the years I've accepted that some stuff is club business, and honestly, if it's illegal, I'd rather not know. We talk about maybe planning a vacation, and how even though I love my job, I worry it's becoming too much for me to handle alone.

It's easy-going and I love every moment. Just the simple act of sitting and talking, is so achingly familiar that my heart hurts for all the time we've missed. I bask in his company, and the simple affectionate touches he gives me. Just talking to my husband with no interruptions, is the most perfect evening I've spent in months.

Hours later, when it's pitch-black outside, Echo lifts me from the sofa and carries me to bed. He holds me in his arms all night, and it's the best sleep I've had in years.

The next morning, I wake up wrapped in my husband. My

nose is buried in his neck, his arms are swathed tightly around me, and he's holding me to him, our legs entwined. I can feel his heart beating and the rise and fall of each of his breaths, and happiness settles over me.

For the first time in months, I feel at peace. He's always had that effect on me. It irks me that this was another thing I'd forgotten about my husband, that being in his arms is my safe place. I can feel his hard cock against my stomach and need starts to build within me. Yesterday, he'd tormented and teased me, and then we'd had sex, but despite the slight soreness between my legs, I don't feel owned or claimed like I used to. We'd had sex, and it was great, amazing even, but it hadn't been the hard, controlling fuck I'd been expecting. Does he still want me the way he used to?

When Echo and I had first met, he'd been relentless in making me admit that I belonged to him, and I'd fought back against his ownership until my heart was so wound around his, that denying him was futile. He was my unexpectedly perfect guy, the one I never saw coming, the one I never imagined would be what I wanted or needed. Back then I never doubted his love or his desire because he showed me. He reminded me with every bossy demand, every unreasonable love filled gesture and I basked in his adoration and control.

Last night, we took the time to communicate with each other and it'd been perfect. All it took was some time and us making the choice to fix what was broken, rather than pretend everything was fine. I feel more in tune with Echo now than I have in years. Finally, instead of being two cars driving in separate lanes but heading in the same direction, we're together, as one.

But I need more than just a nice chat with my husband; I need to reconnect with him in every way. I want him to take me, to own me. Hell, I just need him to fuck me like he used to. Deep down, I want him to bend me over and spank me until my ass is red and I'm so turned on I can't see. Then I want him to fuck me until I'm screaming and so completely owned by him that I'll never doubt his love for me again. But it's been years since he's done it and I can't just come out and ask for it. Maybe he's not into that anymore; maybe I don't make him feel that possessive or dominant anymore.

My pussy's wet. I can feel the slickness, and I cautiously squeeze my legs together, but Echo's huge thigh between mine stops me. I close my eyes to try to calm myself, but dirty, erotic images flash through my mind and I have to pry them open before I start grinding on Echo to find some friction.

I've heard the rumours about women hitting their sexual peak in their thirties and always thought they were bullshit. At least until I hit my thirties, and the hormones descended. Some days I feel like a teenage boy, with sex constantly on my mind. Tumblr porn GIF's are my saviour, and a gift to women everywhere. I don't like real porn; the noise is so off putting that instead of enjoying the show, I get completely distracted by the horrendous and obviously fake moaning. I swear porn GIF's were created with women in mind because they take one moment and put it on repeat. They're perfect.

My imaginary spank bank is filled with these perfect moments and I'll admit I've masturbated more than once with Tumblr on my phone in my hand. My eyes drift to my husband, and my thoughts wander to him starring in my GIF fantasies, not some faceless, nameless person. Biting my lip, I hold back a moan as an image of his thick, long fingers pushing inside of me flashes to life in my head. A barrage of hot, dirty thoughts follows, invading my mind and making my stomach clench with arousal. Echo's hot, wet tongue licking me. His hard cock pushing in and out of me. His hand slapping down onto my ass. His thumb pushing into my asshole.

Holy crap, just the thought of all the things he could do to me has my breathing turning shallow and my hips rolling, to push my wet pussy against his firm thigh. I bite my lip and try to decide if I could sneak out of bed, grab my vibrator and sort myself out, without Echo waking up and noticing. I move slowly, untangling myself from his limbs, but his arms tighten around me.

"You're not going anywhere, Sugar. But feel free to keep rubbing that wet pussy against me; watching you come on my thigh would be sexy as fuck."

Groaning, I bury my face in his neck. My pussy is throbbing, and my mind is still filled with dirty thoughts. I pull in a slow, deep breath, hoping to regain some composure, but when I inhale, his scent becomes overwhelming and another pulse of need washes over me.

"Someone feeling needy this morning, Sugar?"

"Someone only got fucked once yesterday," I snap back at him.

He lowers one of his hands and grabs my ass cheek squeezing hard. "Twice. Once with the vibrator and once with my cock."

"The vibrator doesn't count," I say angrily.

"Why not? It was your vibrator, your replacement for me."

"Fuck off," I cry, suddenly pissed at him, and at myself for my dirty mind leaving me feeling like this.

"What the fuck, Livvy? You feeling extra bratty today?"

"So what if I am? Maybe you should spank the attitude out of me?" The moment the words escape from my mouth, I inhale sharply and wish I could take them back. I freeze in his arms and squeeze my eyes shut.

"What?"

"Nothing. It's probably just PMT. Let me up and I'll get started on breakfast." I try to wiggle away from him, but he rolls us so I'm flat on my back and he's lying on top of me.

He nuzzles my neck, biting lightly, and then whispers. "You want me to spank you, Livvy? It's been a long time, Sugar, but if you're feeling bratty and you need me to remind you just who's in control here, I'll happily take you over my knee."

I blush crimson and wish I could hide my face. Instead, I

close my eyes and pretend I never uttered the word spank. "I just need you to fuck me."

"Are you sure? I can picture the color of your ass after I've got a few licks in, all pink and rosy."

His words and the low gravelly drawl of his voice does nothing to assuage my need. I swallow, but my mouth feels dry, and when I try to speak, no words come out. "Fuck me," I finally managed to rasp out.

He lowers his hand and runs his finger up the inside of my thigh. Reaching down, I try to push his hand between my legs, but he ignores me, simply pushing me away. I feel his teeth against my neck and then he moves down my body, peppering kisses on my skin as he goes.

I silently applaud his descent down, and the closer he gets to my pussy, the more I squirm, eager for his tongue to press against my aching clit. Closing my eyes tightly, I will him to plunge his fingers or tongue or cock inside me, but instead I feel the heat of his mouth as he presses a kiss to my mound.

"Echo," I whine, my hips undulating beneath him.

His strong hands settle on the inside of my thighs and he slowly pushes my legs apart, until I'm splayed wide open for him. Soft kisses pepper the sensitive skin of my inner thigh, but despite my obvious need, he doesn't move any closer to my sex.

"Echo," I say again, the need so clear in my voice.

His finger runs up and down the length of my sex, almost touching me where I need him, but the lightness of his caress only increases my frustration. Unable to wait a moment longer, I push my hand between my legs and circle my clit. My finger touches the swollen bundle of nerves for a millisecond, before my hand is unceremoniously ripped away.

"What the fuck are you doing?" Echo snarls.

"You weren't getting the job done," I snap back at him, my tone dismissive and angry.

"Livvy, you're pushing your luck."

"Then get on with it. You're taking too long; just fuck me already."

"Just fuck you, is that all you want? Just my cock filling your cunt and nothing else? Fine, if that's all you want, then take it," Echo snarls as he climbs back up my body.

He doesn't look at me as he roughly spreads my legs as wide as they'll go and slams his cock all the way into me in one hard thrust. I scream as he fucks me, hard and deep and unrelenting. His face is above me, but his eyes are closed and even though my fingers are clawing at his back, he isn't acknowledging me at all.

Wrapping my arms around his neck, I try to pull his lips down to mine, but he's rigid and distant, despite his cock being deep inside me. "Kiss me," I cry as his hips slam into mine, his cock surging in and out of me at a frantic pace.

"Why? You just want my cock; you just want to be fucked," Echo says between clenched teeth, his eyes still firmly closed.

I lift my head and press my lips against his, but he doesn't kiss me back. I pull him tighter to me, but he resists, keeping his chest above mine, not touching me. "Echo, stop. Kiss me, please," I cry, suddenly feeling tears pooling at the corners of my eyes. This isn't what I wanted. I don't just want to be fucked. I want to feel his body pressed against mine, his weight pinning me to the bed while he fucks me into oblivion. I want his lips against mine, his tongue in my mouth. To feel surrounded by him, owned by him. Safe.

Releasing my hold on his neck, I push at his chest. "Stop, stop, not like this, stop," I cry, my voice shaky.

Echo immediately stops, his cock slipping from me.

"I'm sorry," I cry between sobs.

Slumping back onto the bed, he lifts me into his arms and holds me tightly to his chest as I cry. "Don't cry," he whispers into my neck.

"I'm sorry, I'm so sorry," I babble against his hard chest.

"Why are you sorry?" he asks, as his palm runs up and down my spine, soothing me.

"That wasn't what I wanted. I'm just frustrated and horny—and pissed at you."

His hand stills, and he leans back and looks at me. "Why are you pissed at me?"

"I'm pissed at me too. How did it get this bad? You're trying so hard to make things right and I'm ruining it."

"I don't know how it got this bad, Sugar. I think with the kids and work, we just fell out of practice at being in love."

The air in my lungs stalls and I feel the walls closing in

around me. "You didn't love me anymore?"

One strong hand wraps around my chin, and he tips my face up so I'm looking into his eyes. "I could never stop loving you, Livvy. You are everything to me."

Some of the weight that had settled in my chest seems to dissipate. I can see his love for me and I can feel the way his heart's racing.

"Did you stop loving me?" he asks, his voice cracking slightly and betraying his insecurity of my answer.

"Never," I assure him. It's the truth. He's my world. It starts and ends with him. He's my axis; without him nothing works. I'll always need him, because I don't work without him.

His tense muscles relax, and he leans down and kisses me. His fingers drop to my ass and he lifts me off the bed. "Wrap your legs around me," he whispers against my lips.

Uncurling my legs, I slide them around his back and cross them at the ankle. Echo's hands grip my waist and he lifts me further into the air, then lowers me down, impaling me onto his waiting dick. I feel every ridge of his shaft as my sex engulfs him, and he fills me completely.

Fingers slowly slide up my ribs until his hands are cupping both of my breasts and leading them up to his mouth. His wet tongue laves at one sensitive tip, nipping gently before moving to the other breast. I arch my back, pushing my tits closer to his mouth, while my pussy is stuffed full of his cock.

With a quick pinch of my nipples, he releases my breasts, and one hand slides up my chest and wraps around my throat, holding me firmly. Echo rocks his hips, rolling me along his cock with each movement. He kisses me, his lips firm and predatory. His touch isn't painful and he's not restricting my breathing, yet the feeling of his huge hand wrapped around my neck is proprietary and commanding.

Slowly his hips undulate beneath me, hitting the spot inside of me that has tingles sparking to life. His pace is lazy and unhurried while his tongue slides between my lips, claiming my mouth and owning me.

My eyes fall closed and I bask in the sensation that I hadn't realised I'd missed. I'm surrounded by him; every movement controlled by him. His tongue is in my mouth, his hand at my throat, his arm beneath my ass, and his cock in my pussy. He's moving me and using me, and a sensation of rightness washes over me.

When I'd woken up this morning, I'd thought I just needed a good fuck. I'd thought I just needed to scratch the itch, his game on the porch had started the day before. But it was more than that. I needed him. I needed to reconnect, and overall, I needed to feel this closeness with my husband.

His cock slides painfully slowly along my sensitive inner muscles and I feel the stirrings of an orgasm building. Rocking my hips more powerfully into him, I try to bear down, forcing him deeper, but his arm beneath me holds me still, stopping my movements.

I feel like I need to be in control. I want to fuck him and let the orgasm consume me; but fighting against him is only prolonging my agony. His thumb strokes up and down my neck and just that tiny gesture causes an epiphany to wash over me. I don't need to be in control. I love him, and I trust him, and here in this bed I don't have to be anything other than his. So I allow myself to fall into the sensations and relent, letting him master my body, bending me to his whim. The moment I do, he pushes deeper, and a surge of tingles explodes in my stomach. A gasp escapes my lips, only to be swallowed by his kiss. His hand tightens around my throat and he thrusts harder and deeper. His pace never quickens, but he drives into me, pushing and pushing until my orgasm rushes to the surface and I cry out, my muscles tensing and my head falling back. Moments later he follows me over the edge, his hips jerking as his cum coats my sex, filling me.

My muscles turn to mush and I fall forward onto his chest as he continues to slowly pump into me. All my thoughts have faded to white noise, and all I can concentrate on is the feel of my heart beating, the twitching of his cock inside of me, and the sound of our ragged breaths.

Echo exhales deeply in my ear and his fingers tangle in my hair, pulling my head up roughly. The tinge of pain has my eyes snapping open and I look up into his face.

"I love you so much. I won't ever just fuck you, Olivia. It doesn't matter if I take you quick and hard, or slow and deep,

I'll always want to own every inch of your body. I've been neglecting you and our marriage and I'm sorrier than you'll ever know, but the next time you speak to me like I'm nothing more than a hard cock, I'll make you regret it. Do you understand?"

I look up into his hard eyes and I'm surprised by the heat I see in them. Years ago, if I'd have behaved like I have this morning, I'd have been spanked and then fucked and left unsatisfied. I'm craving the spanking, but I need the orgasms that go with it, so I nod.

"Good," he drawls, his voice now a husky whisper of his earlier dominant tone.

His hands wrap around my waist and he lifts me from his cock. His eyes are heated, his gaze engrossed as he watches himself slide from my pussy. "Fuck, Sugar, I forgot how hot it makes me to watch your cunt drip with my cum. Lay back on the bed and spread wide for me."

He lowers me down to the mattress, and I lean back on my elbows and part my legs.

"Bend your knees and let them fall to the sides," he orders gruffly.

I do as he asks, baring myself to his eyes.

Leaning forward, he reaches out and runs a fingertip through my slick folds. "Your cunt is all pink and swollen, Sugar. You're soaking wet with a mixture of our cum, and I can see my seed dripping from your slit."

His words are crass, but his dirty talk has always turned me on. I should be sore, but instead I want him inside of me again. I've been starved of him for months, and now I've felt what it's like to have his cock in me, I need more of him.

He drags a finger down my sex until he's circling my ass and I shudder at his touch, wanting him to penetrate my tight hole. Two fingers push roughly into my pussy and I grip the sheets, excitement and anticipation building the moment his fingers are inside. But they're gone seconds later and instead a blunt finger probes at my asshole. Right now, he's the one in control, and I know I should let him go at his own pace, but I want more of him, so I push back against his finger until the tip slips into my ass.

He immediately stops moving and pulls his finger back out. "Do you like that, Sugar? Do you want my finger in your ass?"

"Yes," I say, pushing my butt into his hand, searching out his finger again.

"Is that why you brought a plug? So you could feel the fullness of my cock inside your tight ass?"

"Yes," I admit and almost sigh when his finger starts to press at my hole again.

"Did you tease yourself with it, imagining it was me?" he rasps, as his fingertip pushes past the tight ring of muscle.

Biting my lip, I try to push myself deeper onto his finger, my eyes falling closed as the uncomfortable feeling settles and a rush of pleasure replaces it.

"Is that what you did, Livvy? Did you close your eyes and

push that plug into your ass pretending it was me?"

"Yes," I cry, as he pushes his finger deeper.

"How often did you use it? Did you wear it beneath your clothes and walk around our house? Did you wear it while you were talking to me, knowing that you had a plug buried inside your ass?"

"No," I gasp, as he slowly withdraws his finger, only to push it in deeper.

"I can't stop thinking about your tight hole stretched open and filled with a plug. It's driving me crazy. If you had the plug here would you wear it for me?"

He pushes a second finger into me, stretching me further and I groan with bliss.

"Answer me, Livvy. Would you let me lube up your asshole and then watch while I worked a plug inside of you? Would you bend over with your ass full of toy and let me see a glimpse of it, just to tease me? Would it drive you crazy to wear it, knowing that at any point I could push you onto your stomach, flip up your skirt and replace that plug with my cock. Do you want that, Sugar? Do you want me to stretch out this hole until my dick can slide right in? I remember what you sound like with my hard cock buried in your ass. I remember how you like to scream when your orgasm hits. I remember what it looks like when my cum's dripping from your cunt and your ass and you're mindless from the pleasure I've given you. Is that what you want, Livvy?"

I moan loudly, as the combination of his words and his fingers pumping in and out of my ass push me closer and closer to release.

"Yes or no, Sugar?"

"Yes," I shout, blinded by lust and need.

Echo pulls his fingers from my ass and I cry out at the loss. I watch, frantic, as he crosses the room to his overnight case and pulls out a black plastic bag, then walks back to me.

"Roll onto your hands and knees, Sugar," he orders.

I move slowly, my eyes focused on the bag, and I watch as he pulls out a white box. He rips the cardboard in his haste to free whatever's inside of it, and I gasp when he pulls out a shiny metal butt plug.

"Oh my god, where the hell did you get that from?"

His laugh is low and amused. "There was a sex store opposite where I got dinner from last night."

He rips open a packet and cleans the toy with a little wipe, then he pulls out a bottle of lube and proceeds to cover the plug. Using his fingers, he rubs the liquid over the bulbous head of the plug, spreading the lubricant and coating his hands in it at the same time.

His eyes lift from the toy and lock on mine. "Hands and knees," he orders.

I move into position, my limbs trembling with fear and excitement. Twisting my head, I look behind me. Echo's eyes are hooded, and he's staring at me. His gaze assesses me for a long agonizing moment and then he smirks. A tremor of fear ripples through me as he steps toward the bed and climbs on behind me. "Is this like your plug?"

I shake my head, "No," I gasp, flinching at the first touch of his fingers on my ass.

"Settle down, Sugar. I can't wait to see this inside you. My cock's so fucking hard for you."

His fingertips slide into my soaking wet pussy and I mewl under his ministrations.

"Fuck, Livvy, you're soaked again."

He pumps his fingers in and out of my cunt, adding a third and filling me completely. The hand that was resting on my ass slowly lowers, and I feel the thick pressure of his thumb against my asshole. He rubs against the hole, spreading the lube on his hand across the sensitive skin and then he starts to press into me. His thumb easily breaches the muscle, and he pushes in and out, in time with his fingers in my pussy.

"Look at you, Sugar, stuffed full of my fingers in your cunt and my thumb in your ass. You're fucking perfection."

Withdrawing his thumb, he replaces it with the cold, wet head of the plug and I flinch, instinctively tensing against the intrusion.

"Relax, Sugar. You want this, don't you? You want me to push this plug into your ass, so you can show it off to me?"

I shudder as the pressure against my ass increases, but I still nod, knowing that he's right, the idea of driving him crazy turns me on. The pressure turns to pain and I lurch forward, trying to move away from the toy.

His palm rests on my hip, holding me still as he continues to press the plug into me. "It's okay, baby. God, I wish you could see what I can. Your tight hole's stretching around the plug. Fuck, my cock's so hard. Push back on it slowly, Livvy, it's halfway in."

Doing as he says, I slowly bear down on the toy, my asshole stinging and burning as it settles all the way inside me. When I feel the head of the plug resting in my crease, I blow out a breath.

Echo's hand strokes up and over my cheeks. "Fuck," he whispers reverently.

Cautiously, I sway my hips from side to side and pleasure tingles along my spine as the plug moves and a tiny gasp escapes my lips.

"Roll onto your back," he orders, his voice a rough rasp as though he's struggling to get the words past his lips.

I roll over slowly and a new burst of tingles ignites with every twist of my hips. Once I'm settled on my back, Echo looms over me and thrusts two fingers into me, kissing me, and fucking me with his hand until I fall over the edge and an orgasm splinters from me.

EIGHTEEN

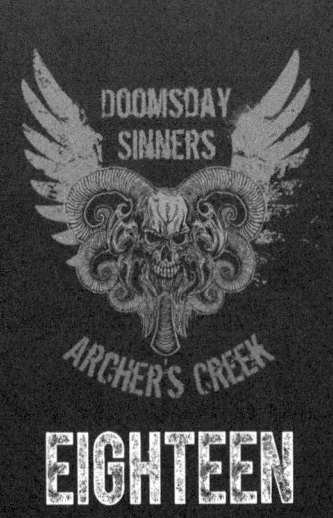

Echo

Fuck me, the sight of my wife's cunt dripping, and her ass filled with a butt plug has me so close to the edge it's embarrassing.

I plunge my fingers into Livvy's tight, wet cunt once more and she explodes, coming all over my hand and making my dick twitch. As soon as her pussy starts to flutter I pull my fingers out and bend over her, stroking my cock roughly until I blow my load all over her tits.

With my hand still wrapped around my leaking cock, I glance down at my wife. Her eyes are focused on the white lines of cum coating her nipples and chest. She lifts her eyes and meets my gaze, then looks from me to the pearl necklace I've left on her tits and back to me again. A smile twitches at the corner of her mouth, right before she drops her head down to the mattress and giggles uncontrollably.

The sound of her laughter makes my heart beat faster and I roll on top of her and capture her lips with mine. When I pull back, she's biting her lips and smiling at me.

"I fucking love you."

"I love you too," she says, a lightness twinkling in her eyes that I haven't seen in far too long.

Neither of us cares that my cum is all over our chests. I'm content to lay on top of my wife and feel her soft curves against my hard edges. "What do you feel like doing today?" I ask.

Livvy sighs a contented sigh. "Nothing. I want to just enjoy the peace and quiet."

"I think I can work with that, but if we're staying in, then I want you naked all day."

"Honey, I can't stay naked all day. My wobbly bits hanging out are not a pretty sight."

Leaning down I bite at her neck. "Don't talk such bullshit. I love you naked, I always have."

"I don't look like I used to," she says, deliberately avoiding my gaze. "You knocked me up three times; now I'm just one big stretch mark."

"Livvy, you're hot. It's even hotter knowing that your body gave me four beautiful kids. I don't give a fuck about your stretch marks. You've been making me hard since the first time I set eyes on you and that won't ever change."

She raises an eyebrow. "What about when you're really old?"

"Fuck, Sugar. I'll be ninety, in a wheelchair, and my dick will still be hard as fuck and following you around the room."

Her laughter hits me like a bolt of lightning to my heart. I need this woman more than I need my next breath. I hate that we've neglected our marriage and that she's ever doubted that I want her. I'll want her for the rest of my life.

Reluctantly, I lift myself off her and climb off the bed. Crossing the room, I turn on the shower, leaving the water to warm while I return to Livvy. She's just how I left her, completely naked, her legs splayed open wide enough that I can just see the hint of the pink jewel at the top of the plug wedged in her ass.

Despite the wanton way she's displayed for me, her smile is the thing that stands out the most. Her eyes are following my movements. She knows I'm watching her and she's smiling at me. I feel like the most important fucker in the world just from her eyes being on me.

My cock twitches to life again like I'm a horny fucking eighteen-year-old that's never seen pussy before, but I ignore it. I fully intend to be back inside my wife before the end of the day, but right now I want to take care of her.

Scooping her off the bed and into my arms, I carry her into the shower, submerging both of us under the warm spray. Livvy wiggles and I lower her legs to the floor, but keep her body pressed against mine.

Reaching for the body wash, I squirt some into my hands

and slowly start to lather up her skin. "I love you," I whisper, as I coat her shoulders and arms in the bubbly foam. "I love having your arms wrapped around me.

"I love these fucking perfect tits and these nipples that I just can't resist taking into my mouth," I say, as I lean forward and suck first one, then the other into my mouth.

Kneeling down, I kiss her stomach reverently and then cover her skin in the sweet-smelling foam. "I love this belly and every single mark on it, because you gave us four wonderful kids. I don't know if I've ever thanked you for the amazing life you've given me. Sugar, I was empty until I found you and then you gave me everything I never knew I wanted."

I reach for more of the soapy gel, and cupping her pussy, I slide a soapy finger between her folds, cleaning away both of our arousals and teasing her slightly. "I'll never get enough of this pussy, don't ever doubt that. You're all I'll ever want, nothing compares. All I see is you," I whisper, as I place a kiss against her mound.

My hands slip around to her ass and I coat both cheeks and then slide down her crease until I reach the plug. I give it a small tug and she groans. "I love that even after thirteen years of marriage you can still surprise the hell out of me and knock me on my ass."

I run my hands up and down her legs and then slowly rise to my feet again. Her eyes are hooded, and she's focusing on me so completely that I know she'd let me take her again in the shower, but I won't. Instead, I turn her so her back is to my front and my cock is pressing up against her ass and the plug nestled snug inside her.

"I fucking love every inch of you, Sugar, and by the time we go home, you'll never question my love for you again. You'll never doubt how much you turn me on and you'll never imagine that I'd ever pick another woman over you."

NINETEEN

Libby

Two days ago, I thought my husband was cheating on me. Today, he's showing me with every word, every touch that I'm all he sees.

I'm basking in his attention and the ways he's showing me he loves me. Echo would tell you that he's not a romantic man, but he'd be lying. He isn't the type to buy flowers and chocolate, but he's not shy about telling me how he feels or how I make him feel.

I'm not sure how I ever doubted him, but then the Echo of the past two days is a different man to the one I've been living with for months. I wish he'd told me what was happening at the club. I know there are things he has to keep to himself, but how can I help him when I don't even know there's a problem?

We spend the next hour blissfully doing nothing. The plug is still in my butt and every time I move, it teases me. I've never worn one for this long; in fact, I only use mine when I'm masturbating. We're both still naked and I'm laid on my side with him spooned in behind me. The T.V.is on and a film is playing, but I have no idea what it is. All I can think about is him. Both his hands are on me; his fingers are running through my hair, and the other is kneading the flesh on my ass.

Since he pushed this plug inside of me I've been waiting for him to take me. I'm almost vibrating with need, but right now Echo is in control and so I keep pulling in ragged breaths and trying not to grind my ass against his hard cock.

His fingers slide between my ass cheeks and he touches the plug before stroking along my sex then sliding back up to reclaim his spot on my ass cheek. Squirming against the cushions, I try to find a position where the plug isn't resting on anything, but it's impossible.

I can't take it anymore. Rolling onto my knees I climb into his lap, straddling his waist and pushing him back down against the sofa. The plug shifts again, and I groan. Neither of us speaks as Echo's hands land on my hips, I can feel his hard cock brushing against my pussy, but that's not where I need him.

"What's up, Sugar?" Echo asks, his voice a mocking drawl.

I blink at him, too distracted by the plug to be impressed with his sarcasm. "You know exactly what's up. I have a fucking plug in my ass, it's driving me crazy, and now you need to do something about it."

He chuckles. "Is that right?"

"Yes," I snap, leaning in for a kiss.

He takes my lips, like I knew he would. His tongue pushes into my mouth, and despite his relaxed exterior, I can feel his need when he claims my mouth, biting my lower lip before he rolls his tongue around mine.

Firm palms slide down to my ass cheeks, massaging the skin and parting my ass so the plug moves again. I moan against his lips and he pulls back, an amused grin on his face.

I glare at him, knowing that being a brat probably won't get me what I want right now, but unable to remain calm. His grin spreads into a wide smile and I fight the urge to punch him in the face.

"Do you want me, Sugar?"

"Yes," I say on a moan.

"Do you want me to own you, Livvy?"

"Yes."

"Do you like feeling like you belong to me, like you're mine?"

"Always," I say breathily, as his finger plays with the plug, tapping it gently.

"You are mine. Your tits, your pussy, your ass."

"I know."

I cry out when he lifts me up and carries me into the bedroom. "Get onto the bed; lie on your side," he orders.

When my feet touch the floor, I climb onto the bed and crawl on all fours up the mattress. I'm putting on a show. I know he'll be able to the see the plug at this angle and I want him to be as desperate for me as I am for him. His soft laugh has me looking back over my shoulder at him and I grin.

"Is that how you want me to fuck you, Livvy? Ass up, face down works for me, but it's been a long time since I was in your ass, so I thought on your side might be easier on you."

Swaying my hips from side to side, I wiggle my ass at him and wait for him to do something. I know I'm teasing him and probably asking for trouble, but I can't help myself. I feel the mattress depress behind me and my eyes fall closed with anticipation. A burst of pain forces my eyes open. His teeth are on my ass and he bites down again, nipping at the skin.

"I fucking love seeing you like this. We're gonna play with this plug a lot when we get home. I'm gonna wake you up, plug up your ass and know that you're wearing it and waiting for me to come home and take it out."

He taps the plug and I bow forward. The sensations so intense I don't know if I should beg him to stop or ask him to do it again. Pressure builds in my ass as he grips the plug and starts to pull. Pleasure mingles with pain and I close my eyes tightly, embracing the burn that feels so good.

"Easy, Sugar," Echo coos, his other hand smoothing up and down my spine.

The plug drops to the mattress and I look over my shoulder at

Echo, whose gaze is focused on my ass. His face disappears from view, and I feel his tongue licking a wet path from my clit all the way to my asshole. I mewl, the sound so feral I barely recognise myself. His tongue dips in and out of my hole and then it's gone, and he's off the bed, grabbing the bottle of lube from the dresser.

Cool liquid drips down my crease and I gasp until his fingers dip into me, spreading the slippery liquid and coating me until I'm panting and pushing back against his hand. Echo pulls me down onto my side, my back to his front. He parts my legs and I feel the blunt head of his cock pushing against my ass.

With only a little resistance, his cock slides into me, until his hips are settled against my back. I blow out a shaky breath. My asshole is full of my husband's cock and I need him to move, whilst also needing him to stay still.

I gasp when his cock drags along the sensitive flesh, as he slides himself almost all of the way out, only to then push back into me until I'm panting and full. Holding my thigh with his hand, his head is angled down so he can watch his cock penetrate me and I wish I could see too. His spare hand is tangled in my hair, gripping me tightly, giving me just a hint of pain.

"Oh God," I moan, as he pumps in and out of me.

"Touch yourself, rub your clit," he orders, his voice barely above a rasp.

Dropping my hand between my legs, I rub at my clit, circling the swollen nub. I dip a finger inside my pussy and start to shudder as I feel his cock moving within me. His thrusts become erratic and

I know he's close. His hips are slamming into my ass with every thrust, and pleasure begins to spiral from my stomach upwards. My breasts feel heavy, and my pussy throbs, desperate to be filled. My clit tingles as I rub with earnest, until it all becomes too much, and I splinter, my orgasm shattering me into a thousand pleasure filled pieces.

Echo's grip on my thigh tightens, and he slams into me once, twice more and then he's groaning against my shoulder, his breath ragged and his hips twitching, as he empties himself, filling my ass with his cum.

The days that follow are filled with touching, kissing, and orgasms. We reacquaint ourselves with each other's bodies and make up for all of the sex we haven't been having for the last year. My body is sated but my mind still feels on edge.

Our third day at the cabin, I lay naked in his arms in the bed. My limbs are heavy and lethargic, I'm sated and relaxed, but my mind is whirring.

"What's going on, Sugar? I can practically hear you thinking," Echo says, his voice vibrating through him as I lay using his chest for a pillow.

"I don't know," I lie.

"Bullshit. Just spit it out, Livvy," he demands.

"What if everything goes back to the way it was when we get home? Being here is great, but this isn't our life. What happens if once we get home and the kids come back, we just fall apart again?" I say, emotion filling my voice until it's shaky and small.

"That won't happen," he says, his voice firm.

"You can't say that. We're busy, we have the kids and work and everything else."

"Then we have to choose to not let it. We have to try harder, both of us."

"Echo, I'm always there."

"Liv," he says cutting me off. "You're a great fucking mom, but you get tunnel vision when it comes to them. We're both guilty of not putting our marriage first and we both need to do stuff to close the gap between us."

I swallow, guilt lodged in my throat, because he's right. I have been focused on the kids and my career. As much as I thought it was him devoting so much time to the club and his job, I'm equally as guilty as him. Neither of us has made our relationship a priority and that's what we need to do.

A tension filled breath escapes me and I feel myself melt into him. "You're right."

"I know," he says, and I can practically see the smug grin on his face.

Gemma Weir

TWENTY

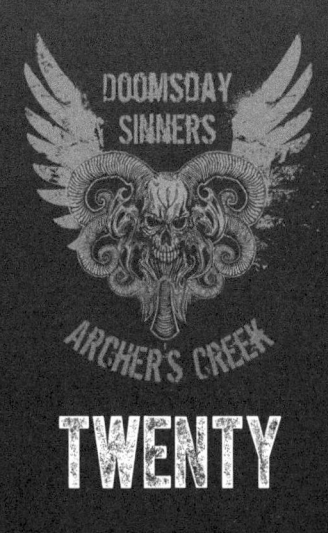

Echo

Today is our last day at the cabin. A week has flown by and I've loved every minute of having undisturbed time with my wife. We've fucked, played, and talked. The talking bit was my least favorite, but I'll talk as much as she wants if it sorts out this shit between us and gets us back to a good place.

As Livvy walks past me, I reach out and grab a handful of her ass. She swats me away, a playful smile on her lips and I realize that this is what's been missing the last few years. We forgot to play with each other. Life's been moving forward at a hundred miles an hour toward a future that we planned, but as the years have rushed past us, we've forgotten what makes us work in the first place.

Before this week, I wouldn't have touched her this casually;

and she wouldn't have laughed if I'd smacked her ass, she would've scowled at me. After seven days unadulterated time together, I want her on my lap or in my arms any time she's near me. I'm becoming a needy motherfucker, because I want her close to me all of the fucking time.

I might have missed out on some years of this closeness, but after having a taste for the last week I won't give it up again.

My eyes follow her around the room. It's time to go home, but before we go, there's one more thing I need to do. Her long, toned legs stride toward me and I can see the gleam in her gaze. She thinks she's about to take control. She thinks I'm going to let her, but I'm not.

She's wearing a pretty summer dress, not unlike the ones she used to wear when we met. I loved them back then and I still love them now. Patiently, I wait for her to approach me and she walks straight between my legs and wraps her arms around my neck.

"I'm so fucking wet," she whispers into my ear.

I smile to myself, dropping my hands to cup her ass. "Is that right?"

"Uh huh."

"Well that's no good is it? What do you think I should do about it?"

"I think you should fuck me," she says, lifting onto her tiptoes and pushing her breasts toward my face.

Chuckling lightly, I nip at her chest, then lower my head

even further. My hands wrap around her ass and I stand quickly, launching her onto my shoulder. She screams playfully, and I can't help squeezing a handful of her ass as I quickly cross the cabin and walk into the bedroom.

Turning her upright, I sit down on the edge of the bed and pull her across my lap, her head hanging down by the side of my legs. I flip up her dress exposing her naked ass and quickly lift my hand up into the air and bring it back down against her butt with a smack.

She screams out in delighted laughter. "Echo, what the fuck?"

"You wanted this the other day, call it delayed punishment," I taunt.

I spank her ass again, my palm landing flat against the curve of her cheek. A red palm print blooms to life and I feel my cock twitching inside my jeans.

"Oh fuck," she cries, still giggling happily.

"Do you remember the first time I did this?" My palm lands on her butt with enough force to make my skin tingle. She cries out, the giggle still there but the sound now laced with desire and need.

"Who do you belong to, Livvy?" I ask, repeating the question I asked her so many years ago.

"You," she shrieks, humor filling her voice.

"Who owns you?"

"You do."

"How long will you be mine?" I ask.

The amusement leaves her voice, and she twists her head to look at me.

I hold my breath as I wait for her to speak.

"Forever," she says.

Wrapping my arms around her, I lift her from across my lap and pull her into my arms. "Forever," I rasp against her lips, just before I claim her mouth with mine.

The End.

Echo & Liv

ACKNOWLEDGEMENTS

This is the book I never intended to write, but I love Echo and Liv so much that the words flowed out of me without me really giving them permission.

Echo & Liv will be my fourth book and I almost feel like a real writer. But none of this would ever have happened without me finding people who support me and have helped me make this dream come true.

Sarah Stanley, I know you're pouting over not being that involved with this story, but I truly can't tell you how much I appreciate all of the support you've given me since I started this journey and I promise I'll be forcing the next book on you before it's even finished.

Andrea M Long, you are my lovely friend, and the best editor I could possibly ask for. You get me, and I'm so thankful that you put up with my inability to use commas and my insane overuse of the word starts. I couldn't do this without you.

Sofie Hartley, at Hart & Bailey, this is the fourth cover you've designed for me and it never ceases to amaze me how you manage to create exactly what I want even from the few random notes I give you. This cover is absolute perfection!

Lastly to everyone who read my books, THANK YOU, THANK YOU, THANK YOU.

If you want to keep up to date with my new releases and any sales or offers, then follow me on social media or join my reader group The Archer's Creek Groupies.

ABOUT THE AUTHOR

Gemma Weir is a half crazed stay at home mom to three kids, one man child and a hell hound. She has lived in the midlands, in the UK her whole life and has wanted to write a book since she was a child. Gemma has a ridiculously dirty mind and loves her book boyfriends to be big, tattooed alpha males. She's a reader first and foremost and she loves her romance to come with a happy ending and lots of sexy sex.

For updates on future releases check out my social media links.

ALSO BY GEMMA WEIR

The Archers Creek Series

Echo (Archer's Creek #1)

Daisy (Archer's Creek #2)

Blade (Archer's Creek #3)

Echo & Liv (Archer's Creek #3.5)

Park (Archer's Creek #4)

Smoke (Archer's Creek #5)

The Scions Series

Hidden (The Scions #1)

Found (The Scions #2)

Wings & Roots (The Scions #3)

The Kings & Queens of St Augustus Series

The Spare - Part One

(The Kings & Queens of St Augustus #1)

The Spare - Part Two

(The Kings & Queens of St Augustus #2)

The Heir - Part One

(The Kings & Queens of St Augustus #3)

The Heir - Part Two

(The Kings & Queens of St Augustus #4)

OTHER WORKS FROM HUDSON INDIE INK

Paranormal Romance/Urban Fantasy

Stephanie Hudson

Sloane Murphy

Xen Randell

Sci-Fi/Fantasy

Brandon Ellis

Devin Hanson

Crime/Action

Blake Hudson

Mike Gomes

Contemporary Romance

Eve L. Mitchell

Elodie Colt

Gemma Weir

DOOMSDAY SINNERS

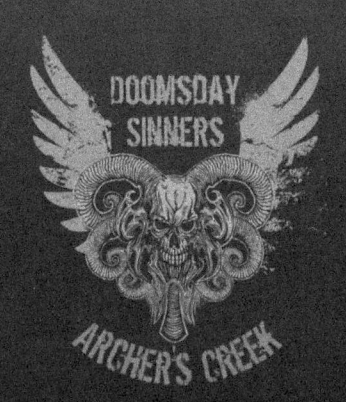

ARCHER'S CREEK

Milton Keynes UK
Ingram Content Group UK Ltd.
UKHW021510140823
426845UK00004B/284